THE LESBIAN BILLIONAIRES CLUB

KC LUCK

Thank you for your interest in *The Lesbian Billionaires Club*. I sincerely hope you enjoy the story. It was a pleasure to write. If you find time, a review, or even better, a referral to another reader, is always appreciated.

Please enjoy!

KC

1

$\mathcal{S}$tanding at the bar in the lavish penthouse apartment, I slowly make myself a scotch over ice. Not just any scotch. Glenlivet. Aged longer than the fifty-one years I've been alive. Life is too short to drink shitty alcohol. Besides, I could afford it. Easily. Twenty-seven years as a puppet master pulling the strings behind Roseland Media, and I am worth 1.3 billion. Maybe more considering how well the stock market is doing. Some of the biggest acts in entertainment answer to me. I am the manager to the managers of superstars of music, film, and a little of everything else. No one makes money without me getting a cut. A large cut.

Smiling, I sip the scotch and turn back to the room. The lights are low, just the way I like them at night, casting shadows across the sleek lines of the black and chrome furniture. An Asian inspired design. Clean, minimal, nothing unnecessary in its function. Whenever I come to Chicago, I stay at the International Towers along the city's Miracle Mile and in this space. They know me here, but then again, don't, because I use a name other than my own.

The world is too small a place to be anything but discreet. Besides, one of the rules of the club I belong to is no names, no titles, no acknowledgment of who any of us are aside from the richest lesbians in the world—a small, exclusive cadre of wealth and power.

In the morning, we will meet. Not everyone who qualifies will make it, but I'm confident most will as there is something invigorating about being surrounded by so much power. Of course, there's always some posturing; too many type-A personalities to have otherwise, but for the most part, the group lets me relax, as if we 'get' each other. Besides, we always have a bit of fun. Someone will always challenge another to a wager or two. It's funny how bored a person gets when they can buy absolutely anything in the world.

But that is all for tomorrow, and I want to focus on tonight. Moving across the room to the coffee table, I tap my phone to check the time, and my smile widens. Any second and the front desk will discreetly let a friend of mine have access to the top floors of the tower. In fact, knowing her and her promptness, she is probably on her way. Thinking of her impending arrival, I feel a flutter in my stomach. The woman is another thing I always partake in when I come to this city. As if conjuring her from thin air, there is a quiet buzz at the door. I could have let the penthouse's butler stay and had him get the door, but not tonight. No staff tonight.

I sip the scotch giving myself another moment to enjoy the smoky flavor across my tongue. My guest will wait; all night if I choose. After all, I paid handsomely for her time, but the twitch of anticipation inside me convinces me to open the door. When I do, I pause to appreciate the beauty of the creature before me. My eyes travel her body, and she remains perfectly still, without a word, as I assess her. Her cascading black hair and mocha-rich skin are a perfect contrast to the blood red dress she wears. The one-shoulder design is as elegant as it is sexy, fitting her petite body like a glove. For a fleeting moment, I think that is a shame, because it's likely I will tear it when I rip it off her.

Finally, I let my eyes travel back to her face. Delicate features. Hazel eyes. Full lips under red lipstick to match her dress. Our eyes meet, and in them, I see a desire as strong as my own. We've never discussed it, but I know I am her favorite client. She prefers women, but not many can afford her, and so my appointments are a treat. When her pussy clenches my fingers, and I feel her body tremble as she comes, I know it is no act. I think she would visit me even if I didn't pay her, but that would change the dynamic. There is no room in my life for a girlfriend—not even one who fucks as good as she does.

Stepping aside, I nod toward the apartment's living room. "Please come in." I'm always polite. Some of the women in the club are Doms, and I appreciate how easy that would be to embrace, but I'm not interested in controlling a woman's every thought. Although I will always be in charge, the butch in me will accept nothing less, I like a natural response from the women I sleep with. Free will is essential, even in bed.

Enjoying the view of her subtle curves, I follow behind her as she moves with an almost regal grace across the space to stand by the floor-to-ceiling windows while I return to the bar. "Champagne?" I ask. She nods without turning to me. Now she too is a shadow, backlit by the moon and the sparkle of lights from the city around us. I have the champagne ready knowing she will want it from our visits in the past. Carrying the flute, I join her in appreciation of the skyline. Chicago is dazzling at night, and I have a fondness for the city's vibrant downtown. She takes the glass and sips. Although we rarely talk, she is unusually quiet tonight. I can't decide if I want to ask why, after all, that is not why she is here, and before I can, she turns to me.

"This is the last time," she whispers. "I can't see you after tonight." Raising an eyebrow, I consider her statement and try to assess how I will respond. Indeed, it's a shame as we are good together, but in the end, I don't care. There are others. Lots of others.

"Then make tonight your best," is all I say. In answer, she drinks her champagne in a single swallow before setting the flute aside. Curious, I sip my scotch letting her lead for the moment, and I am not disappointed. Reaching behind her, she unzips the red dress before sliding it off to stand in front of me with nothing covering her but a lacy black thong. Her breasts are small, but that's never mattered, as long as her nipples are tight. In her excitement, they are, and I already know how they will taste in my mouth. Still, I wait. Clearly, she has an agenda.

Moving toward me, she slowly kneels and reaches for my belt. My whole body tightens in response. There is something so erotic about a beautiful woman on her knees in front of me—by choice. I enjoy another small swallow of my drink as she conquers my zipper and moves her hands inside the fabric of my slacks to slide them down past my hips. Anticipation inside me mounts. I know later in the evening I will fuck her, more than once, but right now I lean back against the window to give her access. The drop is ninety-eight stories, but I don't give it a thought. Nothing tangible, like heights, frightens me. I am rewarded for my accommodation as her fingers clasp the top of my briefs and pull them down to give her mouth access to my swollen clit. I am wet and hard, and her tongue almost burns me as she licks me in a long, slow caress. She is teasing a little, knowing I like sex to be almost feverish, but before I can correct her, she moves in to pull me hard against her mouth. Sucking me. The pace is no longer playful, and I let one hand drop to her hair, where I entangle my fingers to help guide her, while the other still holds the not quite forgotten scotch.

"Fuck," I murmur as my guest expertly uses her tongue to part my lips further and flick just inside me. I realize then I might miss her after all. She knows exactly what it will take to get me off. The combination of her movements from one point of pleasure to another makes me buck my hips against her. She wraps her arms around my thighs to keep me in place because we both know what is about to happen. A groan of pleasure escapes from her throat, and I can imagine how wet she is for me. Her pussy will be swollen and need me to fuck it, but first this—first my turn. I clench my fist in her hair to hold her in place as I come, knowing she can taste me, and no doubt feel me throb. We stay there a moment as I tremble slightly against the cool glass of the window. The lingering waves of the orgasm still roll through me as she leans back and licks her lips. I cannot help but smile. In a moment, it will be my turn, and I will make her scream with pleasure before the night is over, but I savor the feeling of my body as I raise my glass to sip my expensive scotch.

2

White clouds move into a myriad of shapes as I watch them through the eight-foot windows of Zena's yacht. One minute a lion, the next a train engine, and then into something phallic, and I smile. Leave it to me to find X-rated amusement in a simple game. "I see you grinning," Val says from across the giant mahogany coffee table, polished to such a shine I see my reflection. "You have to share." I look at her from where I recline on the splendidly soft white leather of the couch. I like Val. She is old money and has control over vast amounts of real estate in what used to be the Soviet Union. I believe she might own an entire country even but would never inquire. We never do. Of course, Val is not her real name either. We never use our given names. Just part of the security in place to keep the club anonymous. There are too many devices built for eavesdropping from ridiculously long distances. Even with the wind off Lake Michigan today, which blows quite hard for a sunny day in mid-July, we can't be too careful. So, I am Madison. It was my great-grandmother's maiden name, and I always liked the sound of it. I mean, if I get to pick a name, I might as well select something I enjoy.

Before I answer Val, Lila joins us with a handsome young waiter in tow. As she takes a seat with her usual grace, the young man with the tray hands out drinks. They are fruity looking but with a hint of green, and I can't make out what Lila concocted for us this morning. Wary, I accept mine with a nod of thanks to the waiter. I have no qualms about Zena's staff knowing I am there. They are carefully vetted, all sign ironclad nondisclosure agreements, and no cell phones allowed onboard. Not even my own, which is mildly annoying, since I run my media empire from it, but a break for a few hours is welcome too. Once the man leaves, and we are alone, Lila raises an eyebrow. "What did I miss?" she asks, and Val nods in my direction.

"Asking what she is grinning about," she explains. "While looking absently out the window. At clouds."

I know I'm not going to get out of answering so I shrug. "One of my favorite toys, all right?" A fleeting thought of last night's guest straddling me on the bed crosses my mind. My watching as she took me inside her inch by inch. I throb as the delicious memory plays over me.

Clearly not noticing my erotic reverie, Lila immediately leans forward to look out the window at the sky. "Is it gone?" she asks with the playful humor I enjoy in her company. It's incredible actually, how we all act like ordinary people when in each other's presence. I imagine our assistants, employees, and other minions would not even recognize us. Letting out a deep breath, I relax and sip my drink. This has the feel of a great visit. A wash of something unpleasant passes over my tongue, and I swallow with regret as I put the glass on the coaster.

"Dear God, what the fuck is that?"

Lila laughs as she adjusts the flowing folds of her colorful skirt. "An old family secret," she replies, a twinkle in her eye. "Rejuvenates the spirit." I shake my head. Considering how vibrant Lila is, especially at her age, I have to believe the potion works. I'm still not drinking the stuff. I raise my hand to signal the young man standing at attention, ready to jump to any request, across the expanse of the recreation room. As he reaches me, I point at the foul beverage.

"Find me a Bloody Mary and get this sludge away from me." While the waiter complies, Lila laughs so hard she shakes. Val has joined in by now, and I find myself grinning.

"I see I am late to the party," comes a deep, sensual voice from behind me, thick with a Middle Eastern accent. Zena has arrived. Glancing her way, I take in the serious countenance on her face and am not surprised. Zena is the most paranoid of the lot of us. Considering the price she will pay if her sexuality is ever confirmed, I appreciate her concerns. Still, we all try to help her relax when it is safe to do so. Today, she should be especially satisfied with security. After all, this is her yacht, in the middle of a giant lake, with discreet, yet fully armed security onboard.

"You haven't missed a thing," Val assures her. "Come sit. Lila has a special drink for us." Zena walks with her usual confidence to join us.

"I'm not drinking that green shit if that's what you mean," she says. "She tried it on me before you arrived. If it were anyone else, I'd have cried poison." At this, Zena actually smiles and sits in the chair that makes up the edge of our rectangle. Everyone who was able to come is now here. It is a small number, only a third of our members, but we are an elite group and breaking away for even a day, or two is not easy. Empires could rise and fall in a day or two.

My drink arrives, as does one for Zena, the staff obviously knowing her morning beverage of choice and exactly where she is at every second. When we are alone again, I raise mine toward the others. "To good fortune for us all." The other three join in the toast, and as we tip glasses at each other, I notice Zena is looking me over. "What?" I ask after taking a drink, already knowing the answer. I hoped the woman forgot, but of course, she wouldn't. Not only is Zena not one to ever forget anything, but this is too great an opportunity to gloat to let pass.

"You know what," Zena answers, her black eyes holding me in a stare. "You lost. And to think, you could have picked the women's World Cup instead of a stupid boat race." She laughs softly and as much as I hate losing at anything, seeing her even slight merriment is worth it. Zena does not laugh often. I shake my head in mock disgust and hope the price of my defeat is not too high.

"So, what do you want?" I ask. We never wager money, after all, what would be the point? Instead, we bet tasks. "Or can we go double or nothing?" I know Zena has a soft spot for sports bets and there is always something. Unfortunately, she shakes her dark-haired head.

"No. I have something I want from you." I see Lila and Val glance at each other. Clearly, they are in on this as well, and I know it must be something especially mischievous. Cursing myself for making a poor choice thinking the US Sailing team could win the damn Ocean Race, I await my fate. Zena tilts her head, her eyes studying my face. "I need you to stop making headlines. Stop fucking everything and settle down."

Nothing could have shocked me more. None of us are "settled down" necessarily, and although the other three are significantly more discreet in their sexual relationships, I am not alone in having lovers. "Why?" is all I can muster, I am so surprised. Zena nods, and I see the others are doing so as well.

"You're too out," Lila explains, her voice gentle. In a way, the compassion in her tone brings home the meaning of the words more than any shout. "You put us all at risk." I know my companions today are all closeted to some degree or another, but to think anything I do with my personal life impacts them never crossed my mind.

"You're just so American," Val adds. "Everything has to be a show." Again, I can't take offense as I know she means no disrespect. I'm well aware of America's reputation, especially with our latest administration.

Leaning back into the cushions, I shake my head. "I'm sorry. Truly. But there isn't anyone in my life to fit that bill."

"Surely there is a woman you can pick and step away from the limelight?" Lila asks, and I continue to shake my head.

"No."

Zena taps her finger on the arm of her chair, and I glance over. "Then, as per our bet, I shall select someone for you."

"Oh, fuck no." I absolutely will not be railroaded into this, bet or no bet. Zena will simply have to think of something else. Not my entire future. I watch as the woman steeples her fingers and puts them to her lips. A slow chill settles over me, and the air in the room is no longer playful. I look from one face to another. "Someone want to tell me what is going on?"

Lila clears her throat. "If you find some sweet young lady no one's heard of and get out of the headlines, everyone will rest easier," she explains. "Not forever perhaps. But at least for a few years."

I close my eyes and try to absorb what they are telling me. Val picks up where Lila left off. "And no supermodels or movie stars. Someone off the radar. Ideally, someone who doesn't know you at all."

Snorting a laugh, I open my eyes and take them all in. I realize this is just a joke. "Okay," I say. "You almost had me. Good one. Now how about—"

"We are not joking, Madison," Zena's says, her voice cold as ice.

Ever the mediator, Lila jumps in. "Find a stranger, seduce her, perhaps even quietly marry her. Maybe even fall in love."

I rub my hand over my face. This is all too much, but before I can explain I don't fall in love, Val adds her piece. "You have a month until our next meeting."

"Or what?" I growl close to reaching the limit of my patience. The fun and games are clearly over. I respect these women, but I won't be told what to do.

Zena sighs, and I can tell she sincerely regrets what she must say next. I look at her, and our eyes lock. "Or you will be asked to leave the club," she finally says with a shrug. There is no room for argument, so I don't even try.

3

---

*F*lipping through the contacts on my phone, well over a thousand, some of the biggest names in entertainment and music, I need to find just the right woman. And it sure isn't someone to 'settle down with' as Zena and the others insist. Quite the opposite. I am pissed over their heavy-handed suggestion. Using a bet to force the issue no less, and all with the threat to expel me from our group. The club holds many benefits. Financial connections beyond measure, a sense of security as we all keep an ear to the ground of any threats to each other, and of course, the comradery. With a sigh, I know the last reason is the one hurting me the most. I could find others to fulfill my other needs, but the companionship of women who truly under-stand me is irreplaceable. But God damn them, insisting I settle down is crossing the line.

Even after I promised to knock off the revolving door relationships with gorgeous women, swore that I would keep a low profile, they were not convinced. Only by picking just one person and making it discreetly known I am off the market would do. Or I'm out. Fuck them. I don't want just one, and even if I did, the woman would no doubt cost me a fortune. My money does not lure companions who like me for my witty dialogue and clever mind. They all want diamonds, Range Rovers, and twelve-bedroom condos along the coast of Malibu. No thanks. Although Lila repeatedly advised I find a woman who doesn't know me, she failed to explain how to pull that off. I'm too well known, if not by sight, then by name. A quick Google search and my net worth is at the top of the results list.

Gritting my teeth in frustration, I continue to scroll my phone's list. I need someone to distract me. Finally, a name I remember fondly lands under my thumb. A sexy brunette who made a few movies for me before marrying a successful director and giving up the acting business. That she married a man doesn't bother me. I have a fond spot for straight women, probably because it takes a feminine type to really turn me on. Dresses and heels. Satin and lace. This contact choice fits the bill perfectly, and I type in a text. "Busy?"

The pause is long enough to make me frustrated, and I am about to scroll again when a text comes back. "Never for you."

I smile. This I like, and I type off a quick reply. "Tell me what you are doing."

"I'm sunbathing beside the pool." There is a pause, and I wait for it knowing there is more. I am not disappointed. "Topless."

A grin crosses my face. "Need help with your tanning lotion? Hate to have you burn."

"I do need help. Very much. I want your hands on me."

A tightness starts low in my belly already. The frustration of the ambush on the yacht agitated me more than I thought, and this is precisely the distraction I need. "Then my hands are on you. Slippery. Touching your shoulders. Your back. Your ass. Squeezing."

"Oh God."

"Turn over," I type. "Now."

"I am. I'll do whatever you say."

This is perfect. "Jesus, your nipples are hard. I can't keep my hands off them."

"Yes. Please touch me."

"Can you feel me running my hands over your breasts? Squeezing, tickling, pinching. Hard."

"I'm arching my back I love it so much."

She is so damn good at this, I feel a throb between my legs. "I want more of you."

"Anything you want."

"I want to taste you. What is in my way?"

"Thong bikini. Yellow."

As her answers get shorter, I know she's really turned on. I want to make her come. To feel the power of it, and I know what to write.

"I'm tearing it off. You're shaved, aren't you?"

"Yes."

"I'm burying my face in your shaved pussy, soaking wet for me."

"Oh fuck."

"My tongue is everywhere. Sliding everywhere."

"Oh fuck."

"I want you to come in my mouth."

"I will."

I know I have her now. I shift in my seat. I might just come myself and wish I was somewhere other than the back of the damn town car heading for O'Hare Airport. "Feel me licking your clit. Sucking your clit. Fucking you with my tongue."

"Wait."

I do. I know what that means.

"Wait."

A warmth floods over me. She is climaxing. I am as sure of it as I would be if I were there.

"Oh fuck, how do you do that to me?"

I laugh. "Enjoy the rest of your sunbathing." Without another word, I leave the text string and lean back, feeling significantly more satisfied with myself. There's no way I am giving that up. Club or no club. All I need is a drink to top things off, but this particular hired town car doesn't have a bar. I could wait until I get to my private jet, but the itch for scotch is strong after a good fuck. Even a virtual one. If I can't come, I can at least have a drink.

"Driver," I call over the seats. "Take the next exit and find a minimarket or something." The driver doesn't hesitate to put on the car's blinker to do what I ask. He knows who I am and is not stupid. I could ask him to take me anywhere, and he would comply without question.

"Yes, ma'am," he says, and in a moment, we are off the interstate and down on surface streets. It's not the best-looking neighborhood, so I intend to make my visit quick. A gas station with a small store is ahead on the corner.

I lean forward and point. "Pull in there." The man hesitates, and I see the problem. The lot is packed, and there is no place to park or even pull over. As we slow, a car honks angrily behind us when we don't make the light. Stopped on the red, I grab the door handle. "Circle the block," I instruct him. "I'll be right back."

"But, ma'am—" he starts, but I'm out of the car before he can finish. No one will recognize me in the three minutes it will take. I'm jogging across the lot when I realize my wallet and any money is still in the car.

"Fuck," I say as I turn to go back, only to see the car whisking away with traffic. This is great. Now I have to wait for him to come back around. All to go in and get a bottle of undoubtedly cheap and therefore nasty scotch. A memory of my younger days reminds me I was not always rich and powerful. I come from poor roots. Iowa. Someplace I never go. The minimarket is too much a reminder of the shit I put up with growing up a butch lesbian in a map-dot town in the middle of nowhere. Reconsidering my decision, I turn to go wait on the curb when a car horn blasts. I look up in time to see an old, two-door Nissan sedan bearing down on me. I only have time to raise my hands before it bumps into me and sends me sprawling on the pavement.

For a moment, I am disoriented, but when I open my eyes, two things are clear. I have the worst headache of my life, and I am looking into the face of the most gorgeous blonde I've ever seen. "I'm going to make you a star," I mumble. She really is breathtaking with large, slightly alarmed looking blue eyes, and full lips so desirable I suddenly want to kiss her.

"What?" I hear her say. "Are you okay? Oh my God, I didn't see you," the blonde babbles. "I'm so sorry." I try to sit up, but it hurts like hell. She puts her hand on my shoulder, and I am astonished by the amount of heat I feel from her touch. I don't understand how I can be turned on right now when I was just run down by a car. "Just stay there," she continues, a sob in her voice. "The ambulance is coming. God, I can't believe I hit you."

"You hit me?" I am not sure what to think. Is this accident good or bad luck? Regardless, other people gather around me, and I hear a siren. The last thing I want is to go to the hospital. Social media would go crazy over it. This time when I try, I do sit up. She tries to stop me, but I grab her arm for leverage. "Help me up." My words are a demand, and she doesn't hesitate. Even with a concussion, I still know how to make people do what I want. As we stand, I notice her outfit. A yellow waitress uniform. Her name is on her breast. Claire. I like the name. I like everything about her and am about to tell her so, when I see the driver of the town car coming at a jog. The car is up on the sidewalk, the flashers going.

"Get out of my way," he growls and in a second has me by the arm. Even though my vision is blurry, I see the woman, Claire, following me with her eyes. Concerned, but something else too. As I wonder if she recognizes me after all, I am half helped, half shoved into the back of the car and then the door slams. I slump against the seat, my head pounding. Closing my eyes, I feel the car rolling, bouncing off the curb. I let out a yelp of pain, and then I remember nothing else.

4

*F*ive days, seven hours, and fourteen minutes. That is how long it took me to find out everything about her. There are two reasons why I had to wait that long when I usually could have insisted the information be delivered to me within hours.

First, a concussion. I probably should have gone to the hospital, but there is no way I will sit in an emergency department for hours. Instead, I went back to the International Towers, rented the penthouse for another month, and slept for four days. My personal physician arrived eventually, but there was not much for her to do. I don't take drugs. Legal or otherwise. I like to maintain complete control of myself at all times. I've seen too many rich and powerful people fuck up their lives just to get high. That won't be me.

Second, I wanted complete discretion. The search for Claire needed to be handled delicately. No one, and I mean no one, could know I am interested in the woman. One slip-up and the paparazzi would be all over her. I keep a man in my employ just for this sort of work. He's expensive but highly effective, thorough as hell, but the old school methods he uses are slow. Still, they leave no trace of my hunt, so I was patient. Barely.

Every waking moment, the woman is on my mind. But the dreams... They are amazing. I undress her from her waitress uniform and lead her to my bed. Her nakedness is splendid, and I feel a twitch between my legs in wanting her. Yet, even in my fantasies, we don't fuck. I want it to be special and real. In my dreams, all I do is kiss her, because the look of her mouth burns in my memory. A sexy mouth, full lips, perfect. I cannot wait to take it with my own. To kiss her hard until she gasps with first surprise and then moans with passion as my tongue conquers her mouth to claim her as my own. I lightly bite her bottom lip teasing at the edge between pleasure and pain, wanting her to know one of the many things I have in store for her. I stop the fantasy, and even control my dreams, to keep from going further. If I kiss longer, deeper, I will not be able to contain myself. I want her that badly.

Especially now, as I sit with my private investigator and listen to his report about Claire. Claire Hathaway. Thirty-seven. Divorced five years before from her high school boyfriend, a deadbeat ex who ruined her financially. Thankfully, no children. I process the information turning the glass of ice water in my hand as I relax in the armchair across from my investigator. "And does she like women?" I ask with a raised eyebrow.

"A gay brother," he answers without bothering to consult his notes. "Attended Chicago Pride with him and his boyfriend. Not experienced, but I would say favorable." I can't keep the smile from my face, not at all daunted by the fact she does not already identify as a lesbian. At least she is aware of the lifestyle. Less I will have to teach her.

All my life, I have been lucky. Although my success is a result of hard work clawing my way to the top, I know part of it is luck. The right place at the right time. Meeting the right person when it matters. Moments in time aligning in my favor. Just like now. I need a woman to make me honest and to settle down with. A sweet girl-next-door type not tainted by the glitter of fame or hunting for fortune. Again, a twist of desire low on my body threatens to distract me as I consider how I will seduce her. Claire Hathaway could not be more perfect.

After my investigator departs leaving every shred of notes behind him, I pick up a photo of Claire and study the image. She is more beautiful than I remember, extremely photogenic to look so good in a candid photo taken with a telephoto lens. I really could make her a star if things were different. Her body is too curvy for a supermodel, but the overall appeal she radiates would no doubt hop off any silver screen. I wonder for a moment if she has ever acted and then scold myself. She is going to be my special project, not a celebrity for the whole world to fall in love with, although a glance at the next photo tells me they would. This one is taken through the slightly parted curtains of her second-story apartment. I suppress a growl at the knowledge my investigator saw her like this. He's a professional, yet anyone would be aroused by this photo. She is in a towel, wrapped around her torso, and her long blonde hair is wet from a shower.

The picture catches her running her fingers through her hair, her shoulders are naked, and the towel is the tiniest breath from parting. The cloth ends just past her hips, the slightest hint of the nakedness between her thighs threatens to peek from underneath. Fuck. The picture is turning me on so much I hold my breath to contain the rush of feelings rippling through me. There is no way I can go to the diner where she works tomorrow in a state like this. I need to release some energy, or I will explode when I see her.

I consider calling my guest from a week ago, but the memory of her insisting that visit was the last makes me hesitate. If I call her and insist, I believe she will come to me tonight no matter what she said before. I have that kind of power, but perhaps letting her go is for the best. It is time for me to start thinking more exclusively. If I give my word to Zena and the others in the club, I will stick to it. One woman. Under the radar. At least until everyone relaxes, which means no escorts, no matter how fantastic they are in bed.

Luckily, I have alternative ways to help take the edge off. My sex drive is too high not to need to satisfy myself occasionally. Among my toys is a palm-size vibrator, perfect for both partner and self-stimulation. I don't even bother to undress or lie on the bed, but instead, unbuckle my belt and pull down the zipper on my jeans before bracing myself against the dresser where I have unpacked my possessions. Turning it on with my thumb, I slide the hand holding the toy into my briefs until I feel the soft latex ridges come in contact with my already throbbing clit. Sucking a breath in through my clenched teeth, I allow the picture of Claire in the towel into my mind. Forcing myself to keep from focusing on how it will feel to have her beneath me, I let my imagination linger on the image of her slowly, teasingly opening the terrycloth to reveal one inch of her naked flesh at a time. So subtle in her movements, until I see the shadow of hair between her legs. It's blonde like the rest of her and although I usually prefer a shaved pussy, the thought of burying my face in that velvety softness makes me growl with want.

I move my hand pressed against my clit in slow circles, and I know my climax is close already. A throbbing builds from within me, and I feel my slippery wetness against my fingers with each stroke of the toy. Fuck. This fantasy is already a new favorite as I continue to watch her move the towel over her breasts until her nipples are exposed. They are rigid and tight, inviting my mouth, and I lick my lips. Imagining the taste of them almost does it, almost pushes me over, but I wait. My mind can do better, and I am not disappointed as the towel falls to the floor. Her body is delicious, and I'm so ready to come I close my eyes tilting my head back. Behind my eyelids, Claire trails a hand slowly through her wet hair, only to let it continue across her collarbone, pausing at the cleft between her breasts. "More?" she whispers, and this time I let it be my turn to beg.

"Yes, more," I murmur and with a sexy smile, she does not disappoint. Trailing her fingertips down her breast, they graze her nipple.

"Pinch it?" she asks knowing I want that more than anything.

"Yes," I breathe. "Hard."

She does, and the gasp from her throat is too much. I feel the roar of an orgasm build up inside me. As she continues to tease herself for my entertainment, I come hard enough to nearly buckle my knees. A moan escapes me, and I pull the vibrator out of my jeans as the sensation is now too much, but the throbbing from the climax remains—as does the image of Claire's naked body and knowing smile. She is going to be perfect.

5

*I*t feels odd to drive the rented, white SUV. Much bigger than my various sportscars and definitely clunkier, but I want to keep a low profile. I needed a nondescript vehicle to make my approach. A large part of the plan is to keep Claire Hathaway in the dark as to who I really am and thus not influence her decisions. I need her to want me, the person. Not me, the billionaire. At least not yet. In the not too distant future, she will be told, but today I am just another customer at her diner. Albeit one which is about to change her life forever, but that's beside the point.

As I obediently use my signal to turn into the small parking lot behind the diner where I have been advised she is working today, my phone chirps. The sound lets me know this is no ordinary call but is coming over a special app. The app allows me to make encrypted, completely anonymous calls which any government security or malicious agency cannot discern anything other than nonsense. I answer it knowing from this particular ringtone, it can only be someone from the club. Probably Zena if I have to guess. "Yes," is all I say after I press the connect call prompt.

"I'm checking on your assigned project," responds the caller. It is Zena, just as I suspected, and for the very reason, I guessed as well. "I assume you've decided to comply with our request."

"I'm on it," I answer. "In fact, going to secure my target right now."

"Really?" Zena responds, surprise decipherable in her voice, even from thousands of miles away.

I smirk, liking that I am catching her off guard. After all, it has been a week, but she most likely knows nothing about my accident as I put every possible protection of my privacy in place after it happened. Thankfully everything happened so fast, no one snapped a photo or, even worse, took video. My extensive team of snoopers assured me nothing existed of that nature, not that I wouldn't have deployed resources to remove anything from social media. Luckily, it went unnoticed, which is perfect as I am about to meet the woman I plan to make the centerpiece of my future happiness. "Really," I respond. "Update you soon." I disconnect the call pleased with myself.

Finding a space in the almost empty parking lot, I shut off the SUV and check myself in the mirror. I am actually nervous, which makes me chuckle. I never get nervous, and yet the idea of meeting Claire again has my heart racing. With only pictures to look at last night, my appetite for her is simply wetted. Now I am about to be face-to-face with the woman in the flesh. I take a deep breath and let it out slowly to compose myself before I go into the establishment. The diner is exactly like I imagined. Old, cheaply decorated in red, white, and chrome in what was apparently intended to make the place look hip back in the day. The air smells of old fryer grease, and nothing on the planet could make me eat something cooked here. A quick scan of the room and I don't see Claire. Fuck. I worry she is not here today after all. If that turns out to be the case, I intend to make heads roll on my team. Then, I see her.

She comes from the kitchen, I assume, and carries three plates of food. I pause near the front doors and wait for her to notice me. After all, the sign says wait to be seated. As she passes, she throws me a smile, one she no doubt uses a hundred times a day for customers. "Sit anywhere," she advises and then is past me walking to the table awaiting the food. A knot of disappointment tightens in my stomach. This was not how I imagined our first meeting post mini-mart accident to go. Instead, I expected her to stop in place after recognizing me as the victim of her car and the chemistry I felt, even with a concussion, to leap between us once again. This casual encounter could not be further from my expectations. With nothing else to do, I find a seat at a booth not far from the table she is handing the plates to. I'm a little rusty on diner etiquette, but I do know different waitresses have different areas they serve. I must make sure I am at one of her assigned tables. Thankfully, the place is nearly empty, so I have my choice of places to sit.

Sliding across the red vinyl bench seat, cracked and with bouncy springs I know are probably from the original installation, I do my best to wait patiently. I am desperate to talk to Claire and ask her to dinner so we can start our life together, yet the interaction with the other patrons is taking forever. But of course, it would. The customers are three college-aged young men, and they are shamelessly flirting with her. Thankfully, even though she smiles, the charisma behind it is not there. Claire either does not notice the boys attempts to engage her or does not care. I like that about her, either way. Finally, she starts to turn to come to check on me when the young man closest to the aisle reaches out and swats her on the ass. Claire straightens in surprise, and the three boys laugh in unison.

I am up out of my seat in a flash. The fury in my chest is so acute, I can barely take a breath. In two steps, I am past Claire and grabbing the collar of the offensive fuck who hit her. Jerking him toward me, I bring his pimply face within half of an inch of mine. I sense everyone around us freezing to watch, including Claire, and this pleases me. I want her to know I will always protect her. "Apologize to her," I hiss through my clenched teeth trying to keep down the urge to actually bite the little prick I'm so angry. The young man hesitates, no doubt still absorbing the shock of my aggression. He is fifty pounds heavier than me and could probably beat me in a fight, although not necessarily. I am a good fighter, and I would die before backing down. It's not necessary. As has always proven to be true, people obey me instinctively. Even without knowing who I am, and how I could destroy him, I feel fear starting to radiate off of the boy— as if he recognizes a predator when he sees one.

"I'm sorry," he mumbles into my face, and I shake my head while taking him by the chin to turn him toward the still stunned Claire.

"Not to me. To her."

The young man nods, understanding what I want. "I'm sorry," he says with a little more enthusiasm. "Really. That was dumb."

I let go of him and stand up straight. "Maybe you three should go," I suggest, and although one of the young men opens his mouth to complain, the other two override him. My glare tells them everything they need to know about why leaving is a good idea. They throw some cash on the table and then slink off. The few patrons go back to eating, and I am left face-to-face with Claire. She blinks and then recognition blooms in her eyes.

"Oh my God," she says putting a hand over her mouth. "It's you."

I smile. This is better. More like I imagined. "It's me," I say and the same draw I felt toward her before is there, only stronger. A fleeting image of her naked in a towel threatens to distract me, but I take a deep breath and focus. Naked time will come soon enough.

Claire shakes her head. "How...?"

I wave a hand to dismiss the question. "Doesn't matter," I say. "Can we sit down?"

Claire glances over her shoulder in the direction of the kitchen, concern on her lovely face. After a moment of deliberation, which I read in her blue eyes, she bites her lip and joins me in the booth. I put my hands flat on the table to keep them from reaching out to touch her where she sits across from me. "Only for a minute," she explains with another look away. When her eyes return to mine, they are filled with gratitude, and I think I might die looking in them. "Thank you so much for that. With the boy." Before I respond, Claire does the one thing I only fantasized she might. She reaches out and rests her hand over mine. I force myself not to shiver from the heat of her touch. Our eyes stay locked, and the electricity leaps between us. With a gasp, she pulls her hand back and looks dazed for a blink of the eye, then the savvy waitress face returns. "Let me buy your lunch. For this and for hitting you with my car."

Disappointed, I watch her stand up. I can't let her escape. "How about you let me take you to dinner instead?"

Claire pauses. She tilts her head as if really seeing me for the first time, and I watch in anticipation as she licks her lips. I know she will say yes, already deciding where I will take her, and our fairytale life together will begin. The thrill makes a flutter of excitement in my stomach.

"No," Claire answers, and she turns to go back to the kitchen. "I can't." Then she is gone before I even process her words.

6

---

*A*s I sit in my car in the lot behind the diner, I realize my behavior borders on desperate. The last thing I want is for Claire to think I am some freaky stalker, yet I don't want to leave without speaking to her again. Obviously, I have her contact information from my investigator's work, but still, using it seems invasive. Coming to the diner to see her was my way of being polite, only everything backfired when she turned me down. The rejection makes no sense to me. In her eyes, there was a flicker of attraction. I am sure of it. Electricity sparked between us while we sat for the few minutes in the booth. As much as I feel drawn to her, I sincerely believe she feels it too. What I do not understand is her answer. "No," she said. "I can't." Then she fled back through the swinging double-doors into the kitchen, so I could not easily follow her. Of course, I could have because no place is off-limits to me. That thought gives me an idea.

Dialing my assistant, I tap a nervous staccato on the steering wheel waiting as it rings three times. When she answers, I cut her off before she finishes her greeting. I'm too distracted to be civil. "Buy the diner on south 23rd street,"

I say and recite the name a moment before hanging up. Confirmation is not necessary. I will own the place where Claire works by the end of the day. For some reason, I find this reassuring, knowing I have a part of her, at least in this respect. True, she could quit tomorrow, and I'd be stuck with a shitty restaurant, but I don't care. The purchase will have no impact on my immense wealth and power. It's all about Claire. I just need to speak to her again and make her understand.

After another long half-hour of waiting, the door at the back of the building opens, and she appears. Catching my breath at the sight, I remain in my car while she throws a couple goodbyes over her shoulder to her coworkers and then is alone. Licking my lips, I realize I am once again nervous. It is startling how she has this effect on me. For the first time in decades, I worry about being rejected. What happened in the diner never happens to me. People don't tell me no. I have a strange respect for her because of it, but then, she doesn't know who I really am. No doubt my reputation would change things. All the more reason to keep hiding it from her.

Finally, I step out and come slowly around the front of my car. She is at hers, unlocking the door. I recognize it as the one which bumped me at the minimart gas station and smile. All part of the fate which lead us to here and now. "Hi," I say and Claire whirls around. We are only a few feet apart, and I see her lips part in surprise, then recognition.

"What are you doing here?" she asks, but not with hostility, only surprise.

"I wanted to talk to you," I say, my heart racing. "So, I waited."

Claire shakes her head. "For almost two hours?"

I shrug. Although the waiting was hard for me, the end

result of talking to her is what I want. Finally, we are alone, shielded from sight by the other cars, and no one will interrupt us. "You're worth it."

A sensual light comes to Claire's eyes at my comment and only confirms what I saw the two brief times before— she is attracted to me too. I take a step closer, and Claire does not step back. "Why are you doing this?" she asks in a whisper, and I take another step.

"I can't stop thinking about you," I respond feeling a heat starting to fill my body. Whatever her reason for telling me no before appears to be gone, because I see her breath is coming quicker. The chemistry in the air is thick, and I take the final step that brings us an inch from each other. "I want to know you."

"I want to know you too," she says so quietly I almost cannot hear it. The multiple meanings hang between us, and I barely restrain myself from kissing her. "But I can't." Now, she does back away until her body is against the unopened car door. She is, in a way trapped, and I cannot contain my need to touch her.

I reach out my hand, and I run my thumb over her cheek. The contact is electric, and I suck in a breath. She gasps in response, and as she leans into my caress, I must kiss her or explode. As if knowing my intention, Claire turns her face toward mine, and our lips meet. The feel of her mouth is exquisite, and although I try to hold back, I cannot. I crush against her, grasping her hips and pulling her hard against my body. Her moan is my reward as she runs her hands up my arms to take ahold of my shoulders to return the kiss. The primal sexual want inside me rages to life, like nothing I remember feeling before. My need for her makes me tremble, and I ravage her mouth with mine claiming it with my tongue.

Suddenly, her hands are in my short brown hair pulling me toward her, opening her mouth for me to kiss her deeper. She wants me too. As my lips are relentless against hers, I lower a hand from her hip to slide down to the hem of the skirt of her waitress uniform. Slipping my hand under, my palm grazes her bare thigh, and she gasps breaking the kiss.

"Oh my God," she moans. "What are you doing to me?"

I cannot help but smile, knowing she is as turned on as I am. I let my hand continue, traveling over her burning flesh, feeling her tremble, until I touch her lace panties with my fingertips. Moving my thumb in a slow circle, I brush the mound of her lips at the center of her legs. She is wet through the fabric, and a little cry of surprise and excitement comes from her. "Please," she gasps. "We can't. Not here."

I could never be more ready to take her away with me, to make love to her until she is limp and thoroughly spent in my arms. So well fucked she feels me and where I have been in the morning. Suddenly, I realize my mistake. I want her to come home with me but doing so will give me away too early. The penthouse at the International Towers might be a bit of a tipoff that I am not your average woman. Shocked at my own stupidity, I cannot believe I have not thought to prepare for something like this. Especially considering it would have taken nothing but a phone call to put into motion. A small, simple apartment somewhere nearby perhaps, but not a hotel. Taking her to a cheap room somewhere won't do. Our first time will be hot, and no doubt fast as I can barely contain myself even now, but I want it to be something she remembers over the years as special.

Improvising, I kiss her as gently as I can stand while my body threatens to overwhelm my thinking. "Let me come home with you," I whisper against her lips. I mean for the words to be a request, but I know they sound like an order. I can't help it. The need to strip her naked and be inside her is so strong I barely contain it. There is a war raging inside her, I feel it under my hands, but I don't understand it. She wants me. Her body tells me in every possible way, and yet she hesitates to obey. Then, a thought manages to penetrate the fever of my brain.

"Are you nervous because I'm a woman?" I ask licking my lips at the idea of being her first. "I promise to go as slow as you need."

She gives a small shake of her head. "No," she starts but then pauses seeming a little confused. "I mean yes, I've never been with a woman, but that is not..." Again, a pause, and as I watch her beautiful mouth, she bites her lip. My hand, still between her legs, twitches at the sight, and she moans again. "Wait," she begs. "I want you even though I don't know you. God, so much I'm dizzy." I can't let that go, and I stroke her with my thumb again. In response, she puts her head back, and I feel her hips move against my hand. "You make me feel alive."

"Then take me home with you," I repeat continuing to slowly stroke her through her wet panties. In response, she moves with me, and I know it will take almost nothing to make her come. I kiss her neck and feel her heart pulsing through her skin. She moans at the caress. Between nips with my teeth on her skin, I restate my demand. "Take. Me. Home. With. You."

Claire starts to nod, and I know she is close to succumbing to what I want when the unthinkable happens. The backdoor of the diner opens with a bang.

7

*H*earing the sudden noise of the door, I step back, pulling away my hand, and giving her enough space to straighten her uniform. I know we are blocked from immediate view by the cars around us, but regardless, I will never embarrass a woman. Especially Claire. She already means too much to me. "Thank you," she murmurs, and I'm not sure what she is thanking me for exactly. The kisses? The touches? Or for merely giving her room to recover? Before I ask, she looks over my shoulder and spies the unwelcome visitor. Her face pales. I turn to look and see a man walking toward us. From the sight of him and his clothing, he is not someone I would think frequents the diner, which means he is here to find Claire. To make it worse, he grins wide when realizing we spotted him. His dark eyes travel over us, and I dislike him entirely.

Even if he did not interrupt Claire and me in a moment so hot, I was about to combust, I wouldn't have liked him. I've dealt with his kind before. Slick is the word I use to describe men of his nature. In fact, his look is such a stereotype, I'd laugh if not so irritated by his lousy timing. Jet black hair smoothed away from his forehead. Designer jeans, expensive boots, and a black silk shirt unbuttoned two buttons too far. All he lacks are a couple gold chains to fit the look. Nothing but a two-bit punk who wants to appear to have money and influence, but in fact really has none.

"Hi there," he says when he is only a few feet away. "Am I interrupting?" I narrow my eyes thinking of the best way to get rid of him when Claire surprises me by laughing. The sound is nervous and clearly fake, but she makes her best effort.

"No, Johnny," she answers him. "We are just talking. She helped with a customer earlier."

Johnny nods, as his grin fades to a smirk. Any second now I am going to punch 'Johnny' in his weaselly little face. "Sure," he agrees, but the insinuation is still in his tone. "Thank her however you want. Just don't be late tonight."

"Tonight?" I ask not liking the idea she is affiliated with anything this scum has to offer. His dark eyes flick to me, and for a moment, I think he recognizes me. This is the very last thing I want, but nothing on earth would make me drop his stare. If the truth comes out, so be it. I will deal with the fallout after the man leaves. Luckily, that is not necessary. After a beat, he shrugs as if he can't place me and looks back at Claire.

"Big debut," he says sounding proud. "Over at The Golden Rail. Maybe you've heard of it?"

Not from Chicago, I haven't, but I will likely own it before the night is over. "No, I'm afraid not." Johnny fishes a card from his back pocket and hands it to me. I glance at the thing long enough to know the gold lettering on black reveals The Golden Rail to be a gentleman's club. I am shocked my investigator did not learn this and pass it along.

Then, Johnny's word 'debut' rings in my head, and I think of another piece of information in the woman's file. Financial trouble. "No," is all I manage to say as anger threatens to overwhelm me. This bastard is somehow using her situation to force her to work for him. As an escort or worse.

"No?" Johnny echoes. "What the fuck does that mean?"

Before I answer that it means Claire will never work at his place, she turns and opens her car door. I watch in astonishment as she slips behind the wheel, preparing to go before she and I are finished with what was so passionately started. In my universe, people don't leave unless I want them to and especially not like this. Still, we are operating under special circumstances, so I bite my tongue to keep from stopping her. If I make a demand now, Johnny will no doubt catch on. He seems wary enough without me asserting myself further. "I have to go and get ready," Claire says without looking at either of us and starting the car. As if my body is operating outside my control, I can't stop myself from putting a hand on the car door. I am simply unable to let her escape again. Seeing it, she looks into my face, and her eyes are full of regret. Nothing could come closer to breaking my heart, and I want to confess everything, but then she gives me a small smile. It is so beautiful I catch my breath. "It was nice to meet you," she says softly, so only I hear it. "I hope we talk again sometime."

"We will," I promise and let her close the door with a heart full of misgivings. Johnny and I both watch her leave the parking lot, and he stupidly slides closer to me. I smell the thick musk of cheap aftershave on him, and my disgust grows exponentially. In a minute, with one phone call, I'm going to ruin his life, and he has no idea. The man exploits women. I have no issue with women working as escorts or performing for sexual entertainment, as long as doing so is their choice. The Golden Rail does not appear to be that sort of establishment. Johnny is about to have his world turned upside down, and not in a good way.

Without bothering to say a word to him, I move toward my SUV when I hear him clear his throat. "Have we met before?" he asks.

I pause at my car door, not bothering to look back at him. "No."

"Are you sure? Because you look really familiar."

This is the last thing I want so I shrug as nonchalantly as I can muster while putting on a smile to turn and look at him. "I get that a lot."

Johnny nods. "Yeah, me too," he agrees. "People say I look like some underwear model from Italy. Can't remember his name." It pains me to keep my smile in place. When I figure out how Claire even became acquainted with this slug, I will crush whoever allowed it to happen

"I should be going," I say and start to turn again, but he's not done with the conversation apparently.

"You should come tonight," he says. "To The Golden Rail. It's a guy club, but we let some dykes in too. Butches like you do okay in there." I take a deep breath and hold it to remain calm, resolving to hear him out. "I can set up a private room for you, assuming you got cash." I think of the three thousand dollars in my wallet and figure I have it covered. "It won't be with Claire obviously," he continues. "She's too new for private dances. I like to break my girls in slow."

My hands clench into fists. If this fucker is not away from me in the next few minutes, I will kill him. I am sure of it. Still, I know I will accept his invitation, although my choice will be Claire. It will be her first and last night working at The Golden Rail and no one will see her but me.

The idea of it makes a pulse of excitement start between my legs. "It has to be Claire," I say softly, but the look in his eyes lets me know the real me is starting to show through. The one which will soon be destroying everything about him as easily as if he were an ugly bug on the sidewalk.

"Uhhh..." he says taking a step back. I cannot help but take a step forward. The cat and mouse between us is too lovely to resist. "It will cost you three times the usual rate. And she's a rookie, so don't expect much of a dance." He licks his lips again, and I am almost nauseated at the sight. "Or whatever," he stammers. "And no refunds."

I nod, accepting his terms. "I understand. Just make sure everything is ready." Usually, I would reach into my wallet and hand him a couple of hundred-dollar bills to smooth over the transaction, but again, I don't want to give him any reason to recognize me. "I'll bring all the cash I can get my hands on," I tell him, and at this, he smiles. Clearly, he thinks he has the upper hand again.

"Nine o'clock sharp," he says, reaching out to shake my hand. I am disgusted but return the gesture of goodwill. What he doesn't know is I will be ensuring The Golden Rail is packed full of my people, to guarantee Claire is safe until I arrive. I am leaving nothing to chance anymore, not with her.

"See you then," I agree dropping his hand and restraining myself from wiping it on my pant leg to remove the feel of him.

"You won't regret this," Johnny answers while I unlock my vehicle. Of that, I have no doubt.

8

The Golden Rail is what I expect. Higher-end maybe, but a strip club no matter what Johnny and his partners call it. To go with the name, there is a lot of black and gold décor. No windows, or if there are, they are blackened and heavily disguised with gold-colored drapes. The lights are dim with the focus centered on the large rectangular stage in the middle of the room. A signature pole adorns one end of the entertainment platform. I apparently arrived in time for a new act as the woman, who is really quite beautiful and voluptuous, wears a scanty black and white maid's uniform, complete with a feather duster and stiletto heels. Now I know why the place is popular. They cater to fantasy. So many lonely men who frequent these places would love to be a billionaire and fuck the maid. For the record, I have not. The staff is off limits as I steer away from mixing too much business with too much pleasure.

I scan the room knowing most of the lonely men who are here tonight are my employees. I retain a small army of employees, always on standby, to perform a range of jobs for me. Those selected for tonight get a treat to go along with their pay, if this is to their taste, of course. Regardless, they will act the part and keep tabs on anything happening at the club tonight. Tomorrow, The Golden Rail will shut down, at least temporarily. I purchased the business loan from the bank just an hour ago. Not easy as my request was submitted after banking hours, but my people are very persuasive. Moving mountains when I want something behooves them.

Before I've been here three minutes, Johnny makes his way toward me. A smirk tells me he did not think I would show but is glad I have as he no doubt intends to charge me an outrageous price. "Welcome to my establishment," he says with a mock bow. "Come right this way. I have a space set aside just for you."

I don't move, not trusting him. "With Claire," I say. It is not a question, and I watch him lick his lips nervously before shaking his head.

"No, she's too new," he replies. "And not into women." Thinking of the passion behind her kisses just hours before, I disagree, but it's not worth the breath to argue. I want her and only her.

"Let me make myself clear. Claire is who I want. All evening."

Johnny sighs. "Okay, but it will cost you a grand." I can tell he thinks this amount will dissuade me, yet I reach into my coat for my billfold and produce five one-hundred-dollar bills.

"Half now," I say. "Half after I see it is her." I won't allow a bait and switch. He eyeballs the money hungrily.

"Deal. Follow me and then I'll go tell her."

I hold up a hand. "Do not tell her it is me waiting." I long to see the look on her face when she steps into our room and realizes I am the one asking for her.

"Whatever gets you going," Johnny says with a shrug. "But I'm telling you again, you could do a lot better. I have anything you want. Big tits? Flexible? Dressed as a vampire? Got 'em. Name it."

"Claire," I say and wave him forward. "Just her."

He leads me upstairs and through a hallway of curtains covering doorways, much like a hotel. This place is nothing more than a brothel and makes me sick to know women are made to work here against their consent. My breath comes quick, and as I follow Johnny's back, the itch to wrap my hands around his throat and bash his head into the wall is intense. Later. He will get his due later from one of my henchmen. Then Johnny will know what it is like to be exploited and forced to do things he doesn't want.

Pulling aside one of the curtains, Johnny steps back and lets me enter. The space is small, no more than three by three, with an oversized black vinyl chair at the center. Cheap champagne is icing in a bucket near the door and mirrors cover two of the walls. The lights from the ceiling are muted and dim, giving the room more of sinister air then sexy in my opinion. Whips and handcuffs would fit in here, and although I know extreme pleasure can be had from toys like those, I want nothing but the excitement of our bodies tonight. "You know the rules, right?" Johnny asks as I enter and turn around. "No touching her. She can touch you if she wants, but you keep your hands and any other body parts to yourself." He points to an obscure switch on the wall by the champagne. "That's her panic button. If you do something she doesn't like, she uses it." The bastard grins. "And then I have my bouncers fuck you up."

I nod. "I understand." Claire won't need a panic button. She will perform for me of her own free will or not at all. Ignoring his ridiculous threat at my bodily harm, I go to the chair and sit. "You can go," I instruct him and clearly, he doesn't like being told what to do, but he's weak and a coward, so leaves without another word. The curtain falls shut, and I wait in the near dark. My mind races, as does my heart. As much I want to believe Claire will be pleased to see me, there is the slightest chance I am assuming too much. The parking lot was erotic and hot, but I know I can be very persuasive and now the woman has had time to think about it. She might regret letting me touch her. The thought makes my chest tighten with unexpected anxiety. I never feel like this, yet wanting her makes me care. I need her to realize she desires me too, because I know from her eyes and her body, she does.

Tapping my fingers on the arms of the chair, even though it could be no more than two minutes, my impatience mounts. The knowledge I will see her any second makes my body throb with anticipation. Everywhere. Then, as if I've conjured her, the curtain wavers, and I see her hand at the edge. Hesitant. No doubt she is having second thoughts about her decision, and my heart fills with respect for her. I know her outlook for the future is dire, else she would never do this, and I look forward to the day I can assure her everything in her life will be okay. For now, I take control. "Ask if you may enter," I order her. Again, a pause at the curtain, and I wonder if she recognizes my voice. I hope she does. I want her to know what awaits her.

"May I enter?" she asks in just above a whisper.

"Yes."

The curtain moves further, and Claire slips in before letting it swing closed behind her. I look at her while allowing her eyes to adjust to the light. The dress she wears is simple and black, with the zipper on the side. Something short and sexy, yet practical. Like a woman might wear to a cocktail party. I love it. I love that she isn't dressed like a slut, but tastefully, leaving me to imagine what she might wear beneath rather than shove it in my face. Her hair is loose and flows blonde over her shoulders. A golden mane I itch to run my hands through and take hold. There is just enough makeup to accent her beauty, but for the lipstick. This is red and so sensual on her mouth, I am ready to climb from my chair and devour her.

"It's you," she whispers.

"It's me. Is that all right?"

I watch as she bites her bottom lip, considering. My heart nearly stops as I wait for her answer. Even though I know I can seduce her if I choose, I have that power over women, I want her to come to me by choice. To desire me, the person, and not the billionaire. "Yes," she finally breathes. "But I don't want to disappoint you. I don't know how to do this."

Her words are so sincere and innocent, I have to grit my teeth to keep from grabbing her to tear the dress away and ravish every inch of her skin. Instead, I let out a slow breath. "Do what your body wants," I instruct. "I can't touch you. All I can do is desire you."

Claire licks her lips. I know she doesn't even know she is doing that, but it comes from a response to the attraction she feels toward me. It's a telltale sign she wants my mouth on hers. "I'll try," she answers. "But I need you to talk to me. Let me know I'm doing what you like."

My body flares with heat at the request. Giving instruction is something I do well, and I cannot contain the smile playing on my lips. "All right," I start. "Unzip your dress."

9

*A*s I watch, Claire bites her lip again but obeys. Perfectly. Ever so slowly, she draws down the zipper of her black dress. Prolonging the moment while watching my face. I cannot keep the hunger from my eyes and no doubt seeing it, even in the dim light, she shivers. "Can I take it off?" she asks, and I nod.

"Just as slowly," I say not surprised my voice is deep and husky. My want for her is almost overwhelming. Sitting in this chair, obeying the rules, is not easy for someone like me. I live for action, especially when it comes to sex with a beautiful woman. Pleasing my partner to a state of utter euphoria is essential to me. I like knowing no one has ever made her come harder, for longer. Claire will see, in due time. For now, I force myself to be patient as she slides her hands inside her dress, lingering over her breasts, and then pushes it to the floor where it pools around red stiletto heels I only just now notice because of the shadows in the room. They match the lipstick, and I feel my body twitch. I imagine her in nothing but those heels, under my tongue with her legs in the air.

And they are beautiful legs, long, toned, and as I let my eyes travel back up them, I pause to take in her lingerie. Again, I am pleased. The black and white lace and satin of the sweetheart corset top, cupping her breasts, and the matching panties are sexy to the point of distraction, but tasteful too—the combination I most desire. She stands, almost shyly, letting me look at her. The burning low on my body grows stronger.

"Do you like what you see?" she murmurs.

"Yes. Very much."

I see she likes knowing I want her, that it emboldens her. She smiles. "What should I do next?" she asks, and I resolve to let her show me.

"What does your body want to do?" I ask. I must know if she desires me as much as I believe. Claire runs a hand through her hair, pulling it to one side. A self-conscious, and incredibly erotic movement, which I doubt she knows she is doing. Her neck is exposed, and I long to run my lips over the hot skin, to feel the pulse of her racing heart. "I want to straddle you," she admits lifting her chin in a touch of defiance as if I would challenge her decision. "May I?"

I have to work to keep my hips from shifting in anticipation, but I nod. "You may." Stepping free of her dress, she comes to me. The chair is wide, made for this I realize, and as she hesitantly places one hand on my shoulder before lifting a leg, the contact nearly burns me with its electricity. As I suck in a breath, I watch as her mouth parts, and I know she feels it too. The tightening of my muscles under her touch, sparks the fire within me for what will happen next.

"Who are you?" she whispers without moving any closer.

"Call me Madison," I reply using all my willpower not to

grab her to pull onto me. I want her legs spread over me and her body pressing against my own.

"Madison," she repeats while slowly moving closer, sliding one leg up and settling across my lap before lifting the other, until she is poised with her panty covered lips over my belt. She tilts her head, her blonde hair sliding to one side in a move so erotic I catch my breath. "I like that," she continues. Again, the rush of desire to take her hips in my hands makes me tremble. I want to grind her against my body with a passion I have never felt before. Clearly sensing my struggle, she smiles, and I am pleased she appreciates my control, but also her power in the situation. Gently, she begins to rock her hips, brushing against the soft leather of my belt, making the fabric tug against what is starting to ache between my legs. The sensation of her clit bumping me makes her eyes narrow, and I know she is getting more and more turned on by this.

I still don't move, although I am sure I am dying I want her so bad. Taking advantage, Claire uses her other hand to run through my short hair and leans her face closer to mine. Still, she rocks her hips against me. "Why did you kiss me like that in the parking lot?"

The answer is easy. "Because I want you," I admit making her lick her lips. "I needed to taste your beautiful mouth." Now, her eyes close and she tilts her head back a little, moving her hips faster and rubbing harder. "Did you like it?"

She gasps but hesitates. I know she is conflicted because her confession could change everything. "I did," she says quiet enough I almost don't hear. "I so did."

"And now?" I ask. "Do you like how you feel now?"

Claire whimpers pressing harder against the tight muscles of my stomach. I feel the heat of her through my shirt and instinctively, I pull the fabric up until she is against my skin. The move is not outside the rules. I did not touch her, but when I feel the dampness of her swollen lips brush my body, I moan. She feels the change too, and panting arousal looks at me again. Our eyes hold. "I want to put my nipple against your lips," she says between gasps. "Feel your mouth there."

"I want that." And I do, desperately, although I know the act will be sweet torture to keep from sucking her hard into my mouth. She responds by taking her hand from my hair and sliding it into the top of her corset to lift one perfect breast free. The tip is tight and erect, so inviting I lick my lips in anticipation. "Touch it," I murmur knowing I am dangerously close to being outside the lines of the rules of the room, but I need to see her fingers on herself. "Pinch it." I am rewarded with a shudder of excitement coursing through her body, causing her to grind on me harder. The wetness there soaks through her panties and rubs on my skin.

"Like this?" she moans taking the nipple in her fingers and rolling it between them. I see the sensation is intense for her by the way she closes her eyes tighter and bites her lip again. I watch as she squeezes harder, and the cry in the back of her throat nearly does me in. As unbelievable as it seems to me, I am on the verge of coming.

"Jesus," is all I can say, my fingernails clawing into the arms of the chair. I am physically shaking I need to fuck her so badly. A second small cry of pleasure, and I feel the warmth of an orgasm starting to build inside me. Somehow, with barely touching me, this woman is going to make me come in minutes, while I cannot move to take her. The reality is insane but happening. "If you keep going, I'm going to come," I admit, and Claire's response is to lean in toward me to guide her nipple to my hungry mouth. It brushes my lips, and I have never wanted to suck anyone more than at this moment. The sensation as she drags it across my bottom lip makes me unable to breathe. I know then I will do anything to keep her. She owns me.

"Taste me," Claire begs, and I do not hesitate. Rules or no fucking rules, I want to make her come with my mouth on her nipple. One hard pull and her moans come deep from her throat. Her hand is back in my hair pulling me into her. I bite just enough, and now her hips lose their rhythm and start to buck against me. She is close. I am close. And the reality we will come together enters my mind. It is our chemistry, our connection, which is making this happen. We are meant to be together. I feel it in my soul.

Then the waves crash into me, and it is my turn to cry out. I can't stand it any longer, and I grab her hips to help her ride me to the end. As I suck her and hold her body, she comes. "Oh God, oh my God," she chants, and I feel her let go. Whatever happened to make her be here tonight is forgotten, and the carnal need to come takes over. My own orgasm matches hers, and while she screams in delight, I repeat her name.

"Claire. My Claire."

10

We rest together, forehead-to-forehead, while our galloping heartrates try to recover. Still straddling my lap, she doesn't speak, but I feel her warm breath on my skin, tantalizing me all over again. What we did is exquisite in the unbridled passions behind it, but there is so much more I cannot wait to do to her—when she is ready. "Are you okay?" I whisper, and her response is the last thing I want to hear

"No," she says and covers her face with her hands. "No, I'm so not." I blink not sure what to do next. The magic between us a moment before is something I will never forget, yet it will be worth nothing if she feels bad about it. I want to explain that somehow everything is okay, but suddenly she is standing and pulling away from me. "This is not me. I don't know what I was thinking."

As she grabs her dress and clutches it to her chest a moment before rushing through the curtain, I dive forward in the chair and take hold of her wrist. "Wait," I almost beg, completely unfamiliar with the tone in my voice. "Let's at least have a drink." Claire hesitates but doesn't look back at me either. I let my hand fall away. "Please."

Slowly she nods, and my heart starts to beat again. "I'll meet you downstairs at a table." Then, she is gone through the curtain. In the void of her absence, I take a moment to calm my emotions. It is astonishing how strong my reactions are to her, and yet, as a smile crosses my face, I have never felt more alive. She is definitely the one, and I look forward to the rest of our night ahead. A drink. Some conversation. Then, back to my new apartment. This time I am prepared and have a modest place rented, furnished, and stocked with good food and wine. My team worked overtime to make it a reality, and although I have yet to see it, I know the place will be perfect for Claire. Our little retreat for a day or two or more, where we can explore each other's bodies as we began tonight. The thought makes the faintly lingering throb of my orgasm rekindle. The team stocked a few other things as well, and I take in a deep breath of anticipation as I imagine introducing Claire to them. Soon.

"But first, a drink," I murmur standing and going downstairs. The place is more crowded, with a mixture of my covert employees and what I suspect are repeat customers. A curvy redhead gyrates in nothing but a G-string to the pop beat of Madonna's "Material Girl" while a half dozen men stand along the stage. The girl works her way down the line of males, giving each a nice swish of her ample ass and a peekaboo at her pussy, in a quick exchange for a dollar, all in perfect rhythm to the song. I can't help but be a little impressed. Unlike Claire, this dancer is no rookie. As if sensing my gaze, she glances over, and when our eyes meet, she winks. Another time, another place, and I would most likely take her somewhere before the dawn and fuck her unconscious. I know the type. But I'm not that person anymore. Not since Claire.

I scan the room for her blonde head and am disappointed when I don't see her. All the tall, round cocktail tables are occupied, which leaves only the bar itself to search for her. There, I find only men. A couple give me a once over, but my icy glare convinces them to steer clear. If they think I am entertainment, they will be sorely disappointed.

Frustration mounting, I hold back a curse and instead order a top-shelf scotch, no water, no ice. Just neat. Claire must be in the dressing room still, perhaps feeling a little shy after what happened between us. The thought makes me smile as I sip my drink and wonder about the emotions Claire might be feeling. They are no doubt as intense as my own. The chemistry between us is unmistakable. What we experience together clearly has no bounds. Another tug of arousal makes me shift my stance. I am ready to continue what we started, and scan for her again, only to see Johnny striding toward me through the crowd. Even in the room's low light, I see he is pissed, and I set down my drink to be ready for anything. On my left and my right, I feel two of my men shift as well. Johnny has no idea he is entirely surrounded by people who are there to do anything I say.

When he is a foot from me, he stops and points angrily at my face. "This is your fault," he snarls, and I raise an eyebrow.

"What the hell are you talking about?"

"That fucking Claire," he answers. "Bitch just quit!"

I take in the information, breaking down his words so they can penetrate my brain. I am both happy and frustrated. Of course, Claire would quit tonight, that was always my plan, but we had not talked about the details yet. That Johnny called the woman I intend to spend the rest of my life with a bitch is just his most recent mistake. Another nail in his coffin. I made arrangements for his personal and professional ruin already, so, I refocus on Claire quitting. "Where is she?"

Johnny waves his hands in the air. "Left. Gone. Pretty much ran out of here," he says. "And I know you are the reason. Which is why—" He keeps talking, but the words are gibberish at this point. My hearing shut off after I heard 'left' and 'gone'. That cannot be possible. I raise a hand to shush him.

"What do you mean she left?" At this, Johnny actually grins. There is nothing pleasant about it from his shitty need for dental work to the malice in the smile.

"Oh, didn't she give you a kiss goodbye?" He laughs. "Scared her off, butch. And now you are going to pay me the rest of my money for ruining a good investment." A part of me wants to stay and find out what Johnny means in regard to Claire being an investment, but a stronger part needs to find her before she gets away again.

"We're not done," I explain as I tap him hard in the chest with my forefinger. "But for now, get out of my way." Pushing past, not waiting for a response, I navigate the crowd to get to the club's parking lot and scan for Claire's car. My chest tightens when I see the blue sedan washed in backup lights as it reverses out of a parking spot. She really is going to leave. Nothing could have caught me more by surprise and not thinking of my own safety, especially considering she hit me with the same car once before, I run to stand behind her vehicle. For a second, I think she doesn't see me, and I really am about to be run down again, and then the backup lights turn to brake lights. The red flare makes me squint, but not so much I can't make out Claire's eyes in the rearview mirror. Fear. But why?

I hear her put the car in park as I walk around to the passenger side and open it. Without invitation, I sit inside shutting the door and look at her. She stares out the windshield at the brick wall in front of us. It gives me a moment to take in the details around her. The car is spotless but for a Chicago Cubs baseball hat and round-lensed sunglasses tucked in the center console. I like that she takes pride in her car, although it is not new or flashy. She is no longer in the black dress, but now jeans and a white t-shirt, with her hair pulled back into a messy bun. The red lipstick is gone. Somehow, she is even more beautiful in the simplicity of it, and the urge to take her face in my hands to kiss her is enough to make me clench my fists. Somehow, I know doing that right now would be the wrong move to make.

"I'm sorry," she whispers, and before I ask what for, she lowers her head to the steering wheel and rests it there. "I'm not who you think I am. What happened…" I keep silent needing to know what she is thinking. "…I am not that person. I was just caught up."

"Caught up?" I ask, not sure I like where she is going. Things did not feel 'caught up' to me, they felt real. She squeezes her eyes shut and rocks her head side to side.

"I don't know," she continues. "Things are just complicated right now. I can't do this."

Every fiber of my soul wants to reach out to her, take her in my arms, and explain everything will be okay. I can take care of anything which is complicating her life. Anything. Then, I think of Zena and Val, and even Lila's words from the yacht. "Pick someone who doesn't know you." I grind my teeth in frustration. As much as I want to believe telling Claire would not change things, I know it is not true. She can't know I'm a billionaire with an international empire. Not yet. Still, I don't have to be helpless. There are discreet options. "How can I help?"

The offer makes no difference. "You can't," she half-laughs. "You know what's crazy? I can't stop thinking about you." My hopes soar. I feel the same and reach to take her hand only to get caught in her stare when she finally looks up. There is fire as well as sadness there, and I freeze at the combination. "I can't do this to you. Please just go."

"Kiss me first," I insist. "And then if you still want me to go, I will, no questions." I think for a moment she will refuse, but then her eyes soften, and she leans in. Not stupid, I seize the moment and wrap a hand around the back of her neck to pull her mouth tight against mine. The flare of heat at the contact makes me dizzy, and when she parts her lips to let me take her mouth with my tongue, I am truly lost to her. She moans as I plunge deeper and starts to press her body forward until she is dangerously close to ending up in my lap. This is what I want. Right here. Pulling back until I can slide my lips along her cheek and to her neck, I am again hungry for her. "Come home with me," I ask. "I want you."

Again, she moans, this time with more angst in it, and I know the pulse pounding inside me matches hers. She and I are so good together. We belong together. I am about to kiss her again when I hear her sob out a breath. Freezing in place, I am not sure what is happening. "I can't," she answers me. "I need to go. Please let me." With no idea what to say, I release her and step out of the car. This is the last thing I want, but I won't force her to be with me. I watch from the parking lot as she backs out and then moves to drive away. At the last second, she rolls down her window. "You're amazing, Madison," she says and then she is gone again.

11

---

*L*ila sits across from me at the small, wrought iron table. We are on the balcony at one of her many lavish homes, this one in Vienna. Usually, I love everything about this city. Considerate people, clean air, and culture so steeped in tradition it makes the Los Angeles art scene look like a pimply teenager by comparison. I can own the fact that my megastar boy bands, and pop divas are no match for the great composers, which is why I get along so well here. I am not trying to impress anyone. Today, though, I am frustrated and certainly lousy company for my long-time friend. "I have no fucking idea what is happening," I say revolving the delicate ivory coffee cup in my fingers and watching the dark liquid slide along the sides. The unique blend of roasted beans of this modest serving, no doubt, cost my hostess a small fortune, I should be sipping the beverage while at the perfect temperature. Unfortunately, I have no appetite for it. Or anything since Claire left me standing somewhat dazed and confused in the parking lot outside The Golden Rail.

"Because she won't give you another mind-blowing lap dance?" Lila asks over the rim of her coffee cup, almost, but not entirely hiding her smile. She is one of few people who I would ever tolerate taking amusement in my torment, but this is Lila. A more elegant, dazzling woman of class and beauty cannot be found on the planet. I care deeply for her, always have, and forever will. Lila brought me to 'the club' but that was long after she took me under her wing in other ways first. Although not my first lesbian conquest by far, I often wish she would have been. Through her patient tutelage, I learned about art, literature, music, and anything which can delight the finer senses... including how to please every sensual aspect of a woman. Even though our sexual relationship was short-lived by her insistence, our friendship stands the test of time through the tempest of the life of the elite rich. In a way, I owe her for everything that I am, which is why her merriment in my predicament is something I will overlook. I know she teases only in fun, and not at the expense of my feelings. Besides, my private jet has delivered me here for the sole purpose of seeking her advice. If anyone can help me unravel the problem I am having with Claire, it will be Lila.

"It was mind-blowing," I agree, especially considering I replayed the moment in my imagination a hundred times. The feel of her across my lap, riding me, her hand in my hair, pulling me in to suck hard on her nipple, as the passion of the moment swept us away in a giant climactic release. I feel my stomach tighten with excitement at the memory, and over the rush of arousal, I hear Lila's sweet laugh.

"Look at you," she says. "Turned on so easily by just a memory of her." She rests her cup on its saucer and leans forward to put her elbows on the table. Resting her chin on her clasped hands, I see more than amusement flickering in her gray eyes. I see compassion. "She's special to you, isn't she?" As if I am the lost and confused twenty-something that I was when we met, I can only nod under her knowing question. "Oh, Madison. Why is this a bad thing?"

She calls me by my club name out of habit, although there was a time, decades ago, I made her cry out my real one as I plunged my fingers into her time and time again. I like the sound of how she says the word. In fact, I adore the way she says everything. Her voice and the accent so different from my own 'American' variety is one of the things I am most attracted to about her. Some might mistakenly call it British, but there's too much variation to be any one accent specifically. She's too worldly, speaks to many languages, for anything about her to be put in a box as any one thing. I almost laugh thinking there could not be a more out of the box person alive, which is especially surprising because she comes from a centuries-long line of power and money built on a foundation of ritual and tradition.

"It's bad because she obviously wants nothing to do with me," I explain as my shoulders tighten with frustration. "She's gone into hiding. Quit the diner. Rarely leaves her home." I know this, because out of my desperation, there is a team watching her apartment complex. Not intrusively. No listening devices or video. I would never do that to her. She deserves her privacy, which is why I can't call her or send anything to her house to get her attention. She never gave me the information necessary to use an excuse. It's an impossible situation.

"You don't know that is true," Lila says. "But it is complicated, I agree."

I rub my eyes and sigh. "Even if I did set up a chance encounter, I don't think she wants me around."

Lila smiles and shakes her head. "Oh, I disagree. You've overwhelmed her is all. You have that effect."

Normally, I would take her words as a good thing. Overwhelming, overpowering, taking what is mine, these are all attributes I strive for in my life. Yet, these same qualities are backfiring with Claire, and I don't know what to do about it. "Good point," I say. "And that's the problem. The idea behind this ridiculous ultimatum of Zena's is to find a woman to quietly settle down with. Not make another pawn in my empire."

"It isn't just Zena's demand," Lila corrects. "We are all in agreement you need to find a quieter personal life. Your *Lesbian-Romeo* headlines in the entertainment pages make it impossible to associate with you."

I know she is right. Even now, in Vienna, this visit is discreet. We are behind the walls of her estate, far from prying eyes and paparazzi cameras. Even being on the balcony is a risk, sitting out in the open in case of drones or other technological surveillance devices. Lila insisted though. She has less to worry about really. Her power comes from her birthright and not through politics or business. Or popularity, although hers is immense. Everyone loves Lila.

I rub my eyes knowing she and the others are right. After taking time to think about the conversation on the yacht, I agree my reputation could hurt them if I'm not more careful. The time has come to pick someone and stop the revolving bedmates. Meeting Claire seems like fate. "So, how do I fix this?" I ask. "When I can't use all the resources at my disposal?"

Lila tilts her head, her shoulder-length ash blonde hair playing lightly in the breeze and looks over the broad expanse of emerald green lawn surrounding the estate. "Romance her," she finally says before looking back at me. The twinkle in her eyes is enough to make me start to smile. "Begin again and woo the girl."

"Woo her?" I consider her words digesting the idea. "With flowers and champagne?"

"If I recall, you are good with flowers. Particularly roses."

A memory flashes into my mind at her suggestive tone. Decades-old, but the image of Lila's naked slender body laid out before me on a bed of white satin is still fresh in my memory. Blood red rose petals are everywhere. All part of a clumsy attempt by the younger me to be romantic and please her. As unoriginal as it was, she embraced the moment and handed me one of the flowers on its long stem. "Touch me with this," she instructed, always with the same knowing smile. Not sure what she meant, I started to ask, but she put a finger to my lips. "Don't think so much, my love, follow your instincts."

Holding my breath in concentration as much as arousal, I took the rose and leaned over her to tentatively trace the velvety red petals across her cheek. As I watched, she closed her eyes and sighed. Encouraged, I moved slowly down her neck, across her shoulder, to her small breasts, stopping at the tight nipples to tease and was rewarded with a moan. "Keep going," she whispered, and I slipped the flower lower. Trailing along her flat stomach, to the neat patch of hair between her legs, where I stood at the ready, strap-on harnessed around my hips and thighs. Feeling more confident as she arched her back in anticipation of my caress, I slid the rose along the inside of her thigh, with the lightest brush against her hard clit. Her gasp taught me the lesson I knew she intended, just as I know her reminding me of that moment is a lesson as well. Sometimes the gentlest touch can be the perfect preparation for the intensity to come. In life as well as sex.

"Okay," I acknowledge. "I can do that."

Lila picks up her coffee and holds the cup to her lips. "Oh, I know you can."

12

*R*omancing I can do, especially for Claire, as my emotions demand it, but drawing the woman out is the challenge. For four days, the furthest she ventured out was the small grocery store on the corner of her block to buy fresh fruits, vegetables, and of all things, gin and black pepper. My opportunities to woo her are thereby ridiculously limited. Only after hours of pacing the penthouse am I able to come up with a plan which might work. The night at The Golden Rail when I was in her car, there was a Chicago Cubs baseball cap. I recall it vividly as the memorabilia held almost a place of reverence among the otherwise spotless interior. If she is a diehard fan of the team, I know I might have a chance. All I need to do is get her a ticket to the next game and bump into her at the stadium.

Securing the prime location of the seat was essential. I went with a good, but not great, seat on the home team's side, field level. Next, to get the ticket into her possession. A quick discussion with the counter clerk at the little store she frequented, and a promise to change his life and that of his family's forever, convinced him to present the baseball ticket to her as a favor. Watching the store's video surveillance footage later, I realize how close he and I came to failing our mission. Claire simply could not believe the ticket was available and for free. The clerk begged her to believe he had an extra and because she was so nice to him all the time, she could have it if she wanted. In the end, Claire caved.

Which is why I am standing in one of the many venue halls of Wrigley Field in a Cubs hat of my own, with dark sunglasses, and praying the people milling by me don't recognize me. Any minute now, Claire should be walking by on her way to the seat. My heart beats a million miles a second knowing I will see her again. She has consumed my thoughts and my dreams. I focus on nothing else but her since we met, and others are noticing. My business colleagues are starting to inquire as to my health, but how do I explain I am lovesick.

Then, there she is, and I freeze. The baseball hat tries but fails to contain her flowing blonde hair, while her faded Chicago Cubs T-shirt hugs her body perfectly. A small backpack hangs from her shoulder. Jeans with holes at the knee, sandals, and the round sunglasses, complete her outfit, and I am captivated. Taking a deep breath, I start walking, and it is easy to intercept her as she looks at her phone. Our shoulders bump.

"Oh God, I am so sorry," she apologizes looking up to see who she has run into this time. I watch as the moment registers. "No. This is impossible."

I smile as innocently as I can muster, which feels utterly alien on my face, but for her, I will try anything. "It was my fault. I wasn't looking."

She shakes her head. "No, I mean impossible you are here. Right here."

At this, I shrug. "I like baseball." This is partially true. I strongly considered buying an MLB franchise in Tampa not long ago. Taking a deep breath, I forage on. "It's good to see you."

Her face softens. "You too," she says. "I'm sorry about the other night." My heart skips a beat at this confession. Perhaps she has thought of me after all and what we shared, the intensity of our touches. All of it.

"It's okay," is all I think to mutter and am ready to kick myself for not handling this better. My empire requires me to interact with the most influential people on the planet, and yet I can't seem to have a normal conversation in this instance. We stand together, a bit awkward, as the silence lingers.

"Well, I think I better find my seat," she says still not turning away and I nod, almost missing the fact this is my cue. The woman does something to my brain, I swear. Pulling my own ticket from the back pocket of my jeans, I make a show of checking my assigned location.

"Where are you sitting?" I ask. Claire mimics my movement, and in a second, we both consider where we will sit. My seat is purposefully an entire section over from hers, closer to the field, and a prime spot. In fact, I've purchased it as well as the whole row to ensure no distractions.

"Great spot." She smiles. "Maybe catch a foul ball even."

This is my chance, and my heart races like I'm a teenager about to ask my first girl to a high school dance. "I have an extra ticket. My friend canceled last minute. Sit with me?"

Watching her face, while holding my breath, Claire bites her lip, but only hesitates a moment. "Are you sure?"

"Yes," I breathe. "It will be fun." Before I say more, a cheer erupts from the crowd. The Cubs are taking the field. "We should go sit down."

Claire smiles slipping her hand through my arm so we

can walk together. I know it is meant to be casual and friendly, but the contact nearly freezes me on the spot, and I see her hesitate too. She feels the electricity running between us. Sitting beside her is going to be sweet torture, and I am pleased to think it will be that way for both of us. She wants me; I can feel it.

The seats are truly excellent, and if she notices we are basically alone, she doesn't mention it. In the past, I've attended professional baseball games, always from luxury boxes as a guest to the team's owners or other influential people related to or fans of the sport. Generally, I disregard the actual events happening on the field. I'm not there for the game, but to do business. Make deals. Forward my agenda. Now though, as I sit beside a true fan, I am captivated by both the action unfolding as well as her enthusiasm. If I envisioned a quiet and tender romantic moment beside the woman I can't stop fantasizing about, I was off the mark. Each play, whether the Cubs are in the field or batting, requires her opinion on its quality. Somehow, I find it charming to see her jump from her seat to cheer a particularly impressive feat of athleticism.

As the first inning ends, she plops back down, cheeks flushed, and I am captivated. "Did you see that?" she asks breathless, a light of fervor in her eyes. "I swear, if our shortstop doesn't make the All-Star team, I'm going to be pissed." Suddenly, she stops, her mouth in an O, as she seems to realize how she is acting and what she just said. I laugh because it's so endearing on her beautiful face.

"I saw," I reply not talking at all about the Cubs defense but rather her. The passion in her abounds, and I feel my body tighten as I look forward to channeling it. Perhaps sensing my distraction at her ardor, she catches me off-guard.

"You're not really a Cubs fan, are you," she states.

It is not a question, and I swallow to buy a second, but in the end, I fess up. "I am now."

She tilts her head, blonde hair cascading over her shoulder, and I force myself not to reach for it—to run my hand through it, clasp it and pull her into me. Her next question snaps me back to the moment. "How do I know this mysterious ticket Rashid magically had for me has something to do with you?"

"I don't know what you are talking about," is the best I can come up with under this sudden scrutiny. I am a fool to think she would not see through my weak attempt to meet her again. "Who's Rashid?"

"A good friend at the counter of the store I go to a lot. He gave me the ticket."

I pause. The idea of blatantly lying to her does not sit well with me. I am at a crossroads, and the time has arrived where I must confess both who I am and what she means to me. Taking a deep breath, I open my mouth to begin when she shakes her head.

"No, that's impossible," she says for the second time tonight, more to herself than to me. This feels like a really good time to stay quiet, so I wait, and after a moment, she laughs and turns her attention back to the game. Another inning begins. "Well, since you're new to the experience, let me show you how to be a true Cubs fan." Before I respond, she whistles to flag down the stadium vendor walking the stands carrying peanuts and beer. "First, we need nourishment."

I cannot help but laugh. She is infectious and, at this moment, I am a new baseball fan.

13

By the seventh-inning stretch, I am hooked on the game. According to Claire, the team we are playing, the evil Cardinals, are the archrivals and the crowd reinforces this. Everyone is standing by the end of the Cubs latest at bat, where they have blown the game wide open with a six-run inning. After the last runner is tagged out and the action stops for a moment, Claire sinks back to her chair, and I join her. "This is incredible," I admit, and she laughs. I love the sound, so carefree and authentic, that at this moment, I have to join in. When we sober at last, she surprises me by touching my cheek while staring into my eyes. The heat of her hand makes me shiver with attraction. Still, her look is serious, so I subdue my almost desperate urge to kiss her.

"I know you did this. I don't know how, but I know you did."

I will not lie to her outright, but she doesn't need to know all the details yet, so I only nod as I take her hand in mine. This time, she is the one who reacts to the touch, and I watch her bite her bottom lip awaiting my answer.

"I just wanted to see you again," I admit. "I needed to."

"I needed it too," she agrees, leaning closer, sliding her other hand along my leg, touching my thigh. Fire blooms through me, and I want her so bad it hurts. Over the roar of passion in my ears, I faintly hear the game starting up again, and pray she won't notice for another moment, so I can kiss her. I am hungry for her and do not hesitate.

The touch of our lips is electric, and only the fact we are in a public place slows my impulse to ravish her mouth. Before we deepen the embrace, the sound of a bat on a ball echoes from the field, and we break apart. "To be continued," she murmurs against my lips, and as frustrated as I am at stopping now, I like the sound of that. A lot.

The rest of the game is a blur as I think about what Claire meant and what is coming next for us. When the game ends, with a Cubs win, the victory has Claire on high, bouncing along as we walk out of the stands, hanging onto my arm. As we reach the top of the stairs, she kisses my cheek.

"What's that for?" I ask, and she shrugs smiling broadly.

"Just for everything. I know this had to cost you a fortune, and I appreciate it. I'll never forget tonight."

I think Lila would approve of my progress and I smile. "I won't forget it either. And you've made me a Cubs fan."

"I think I have!" She laughs, and we head out the stadium's front gate to stand on the sidewalk. Things are suddenly awkward. I am ready to take her home with me, possibly forever, but I remind myself Claire deserves more. I must charm her, yet my body throbs with the desire to take her to bed.

"Dinner?" I offer needing to prolong the date so the woman can't slip out of my life yet again. Claire looks at me, a mixture of emotions in her eyes. I am unable to read all of them, but two are clearly desire and regret. Both make me long to reach for her and pull her closer, to make everything okay for her. Before I move, she shakes her head, breaking my heart a little.

"I should go," she says, starting to back away down the sidewalk. I can't let this happen again.

"Wait. How did you get here?" I already know the answer. She took the train, and the closest stop is six blocks away from the stadium, but perhaps I can get her to let me drive her home. "Can I give you a lift?" Again, the hesitation. I see in her eyes she wants to say yes, but something I don't know about worries her. Nothing could be more frustrating as my investigator has not yet determined what holds her back. "I promise to behave," I add holding up my hands in an innocent gesture. "Just a ride home."

"Okay," she agrees with a nod, a hint of relief but also something else on her face. I can't read it, but then she is linking arms with me again, and we are moving toward the parking structure across the street. "Just a ride home." The sentence is a whisper, and I wonder if she is saying it to remind me or convince herself. I resolve on the spot to restrain myself no matter what happens and let Claire make the next move. As much as I crave control, Lila's words remind me to not overwhelm the woman who walks in silence beside me. The phrase, patience is a virtue, comes to mind.

I am considering how long the wait might be, or if she will ever come to me at all when we enter the parking garage elevator. The car is only half full, and because I parked on the roof, away from others for security reasons, it quickly empties while we ascend. After three stops, we are alone. Before I consider the possibilities of what I could do to Claire in this elevator, she grabs my face in both hands and kisses me. I recover from my surprise quickly and let my mouth cover hers wanting to consume her. I am rewarded with a moan, but even more incredible is the feel of her tongue tickling my lips, searching for mine. Now I am the one who growls as I respond in kind and plunge into her mouth to claim it. She shivers, and the woman's want for me radiates off her skin, as I feel her hands push into my hair, knocking the baseball cap from my head, while she pulls me harder into the kiss.

Only the sound of the elevator doors chiming at our level breaks into our passion. "Car," she gasps against my lips and with hands all over each other, we stumble to my SUV. I press her up against the side of the vehicle with my body and retake her mouth. She is as eager as I am, and the sensation thrills me. Typically, I want submissive and compliant, but her tongue darting into my mouth to tempt me, causes a fire to start within my body like no other. Our lips are hard against each other, a moan escapes my throat, and I cannot get enough of her mouth. Her hands grasp my shirt and hold me against her. Her legs part letting me shift to slip my thigh between them. The contact of my muscle against her makes her cry out against my lips, breaking the kiss. "Jesus," she gasps. "I want you."

I don't know what happened to the shy girl from The Golden Rail. Perhaps in the excitement of the game, the adrenaline of winning, her passion is unbridled, but the answer doesn't matter. I want her just as much. "I need to taste you," is my response, and she shudders with desire.

"I need that too."

I fumble for the keys and press the button to unlock the

doors. Grabbing for the door handle to the back seat, I yank the door open, and together we tumble inside. I am on top of her, my hips between her legs. The urge to thrust is strong, but I wait. This is not the time for that, and after I reach back to drag the door closed, thankful for the tinted windows, I turn back to see Claire unbuttoning her jeans. I watch in pleased astonishment as she pulls them open and I see a hint of black lace panties beneath. Her want is shining in her eyes, and a hunger to bury my mouth between her legs overwhelms me. I grab the waist of her jeans and rip them down off her hips. The panties come with them, and I see her nakedness in the dim light. Never have I wanted to suck a woman's clit more, and I lower my body, so my mouth is poised just above her. She squirms with impatience, and I love it.

"I'm going to taste you, Claire," I murmur. "And fuck you with my tongue, until you can't stand it." Claire arches her back in response.

"Yes," she moans. "Please." I pause. There is a hint of desperation in her voice. Both erotic, but something else too. A sense of abandon, as if this might be the last time for her. If that is somehow the case, and I swear it will not be, I intend to make her come so hard she remembers this night forever.

Lowering myself, I let my tongue part her lips and find her clit. It is hard, and I know it must be throbbing. A long slow glide across it and Claire bucks up against my face as a whimper comes from her throat. I smile and do it again, harder this time. I am rewarded with an "Oh, God," from her, and I take this as a sign to wrap my lips around her clit and slowly suck. I move my head side-to-side, building friction, as she continues to squirm and buck under my mouth.

I suck harder, faster and hear her breathing grow ragged. She is close. I know from her body and by her desperate sounds. "Yes," she cries, and I move faster against her. "Oh, yes. Yes." Then a cry rips from her throat and her back arches as she rides the waves of orgasm. Nothing could please me more.

14

$\mathcal{I}$ will never forget the look on Claire's face as I pull into the valet circle at the International Towers. This is not something she could have ever predicted, and frankly, until ten minutes ago, I would not have guessed it either. But my fake apartment is too far away to wait while my pulse pounds with the need to continue with Claire. I did not dare let her reconsider her answer. When I whispered, "Come home with me," into her neck as we both tried to catch our breath in the back of the car, I could feel her body tense at my request, but I was not to be deterred. "You know this isn't done." I felt her nod against my cheek, and so here we are.

The valets jump when they recognize me through the windshield, and as they open the car doors, I hold up a hand to silence them. Now is not the time to reveal to Claire exactly who I am. She looks overwhelmed as it is, and I will explain it all later. For now, I put on my baseball cap and sunglasses. Claire follows my lead and taking her arm, we hurry through the lobby to the special elevator. I don't exhale until we are safely inside.

"Who in the hell are you?" she asks sounding a mixture of fascinated and angry. My answer is to quiet her with a kiss. The passion flows between us, and I feel her relax into me as my tongue explores her mouth. When we reach the top floor, I pull back and stare into her eyes.

"For now, I'm just Madison," I instruct her, and thankfully, she doesn't say another word as we step into the penthouse. Claire stops just inside, and I pause with her.

"My God, this is fantastic," she murmurs, and I look at the space with fresh eyes. The vastness of the room truly is beautiful in its décor. Luxury everywhere. But mostly, I am drawn to the windows where the sun has gone down and the lights of the city dazzle. "How—" I put a finger to her lips, and our eyes meet.

"It's just us for tonight," I tell her, and she furrows her brow. I can tell she has a million questions, but I am not ready for our date to be over yet. "I will answer anything you ask in the morning. Okay?" A look of something passes through her eyes; regret again, and I am reminded I want to know more about her, too. "We will talk."

She sighs. "Yes," she agrees and lets me take her hand to lead her to the windows. The view is spectacular, as always. "Breathtaking," I hear her say before she turns to look at me. I know she wants to ask me who I am again. It is evident in her eyes, but after a moment, she simply nods and steps closer inviting a kiss.

My mouth finds hers, and the intense fever from before quickly returns. She is willing to leave all questions for tonight alone, and as I grab her hips to pull her into me, she gasps. "Wait," she breathes. "Where's the bathroom?" I smile and tip my head in the bathroom's direction across the giant suite. After another sultry kiss, she goes leaving me to make myself a scotch and consider what I am doing. The sudden impulse to bring her here has me conflicted. This is far sooner than I planned yet feels right. In fact, everything about Claire feels right. Almost so much, it makes me uneasy. I can accept my fascination with the woman and my need to seduce her, but the other emotions... I'll think about those later.

Drink in hand, I move to the giant couch and wait. The image of her under me, after I pleased her with my mouth, stirs my hunger again. My need for release is building, and I sip my drink to try to relax while I wait. All in due time. Nevertheless, I already know I will come hard once that time does arrive. Claire does something to me I can't explain. Heightens my responses to the slightest touch. I shiver thinking of what I want to do with her tonight.

I hear the door to the bathroom suite open and turn to look. My eyes widen at the sight. Claire is in a white robe, and it hangs slightly open to reveal her black lace bra and matching panties. I lick my lips as she crosses the room to stand before me. I see her nervousness has returned, the rush from the ballgame gone, and now she is in my lair. This woman is my prey, and she knows it.

"You look amazing," I say setting my drink on the coffee table and standing up to go to her. Our mouths meet again, and I kiss her deeply as she slips her arms around my neck. Sliding my hands under the robe, I relish the hot bare skin I find and pull her against me. The moan from her throat makes me throb, and I want to take her into the bedroom already. I force myself to slow down and enjoy the feel of her body. The curve of her hip, the tightness of her stomach, the swell of her breast. My thumb slips under the fabric of the bra and brushes her tight nipple. She shivers, and I pinch gently this time, which makes her whimper with desire in my mouth. So many things I want to do to her, and my instinct tells me she will love them all.

I trail my hand down her body, letting my fingertips skim the surface of her burning skin until I am at the edge of her panties. With my mouth still on hers, I slip under the lace and she trembles. I shift and trail my lips down her jawline to her neck. I feel the pulse of her racing heart there and nip it gently. "Are you wet?" I whisper, and she gasps.

"So wet."

In response, I slide my finger down between her lips, and she is indeed— as well as swollen and ready for me. I keep going, letting my other finger skim over her hard clit until I am sliding inside her. I suck in a breath. She is so tight, so hot, I feel my body responding with wetness of my own between my legs. The need to fuck her is intense, but I grit my teeth to keep my movements slow. Another stroke in and out. "Oh God," she whispers, and I feel her tighten around my finger. The sensation makes me close my eyes, and I answer with another, deeper thrust. She rests against me for support as I slip in and out of her. Again. And again. Slow, steady, drawing out her pleasure. Her breath starts to come faster, and I respond with a second finger. Her body quivers at the fullness, and I go deeper looking for a specific spot. Curling my fingers a little, I find the smoothness I want and slide over it, pressing harder. With a cry of surprise and pleasure, she grabs my shirt and grinds against me. "What are you doing?" she asks looking into my eyes as I do it again. This time her entire body bucks. "That's so incred—" I interrupt her with another stroke, and the look in her eyes is priceless. I know no one has touched her G-spot before and that her orgasm will be like no other.

"Come for me," I tell her as I continue my caress inside her. Her mouth opens to say something else, but no words come out when I go again. Her eyes close, and her body shakes. My other arm wraps tight around her waist to hold her up and pressed against me. She trembles under my touch. Once more, I caress her, and she cries out. Once. Twice. I feel the walls of her start to quiver around my fingers, and I feel intense satisfaction. She is starting to come. I know it will be hard, and she cries out again. Louder. A small scream of pleasure rages from her core, followed by another. The intensity makes her out of control. One more stroke and as she screams again, I feel her release completely, wetness coats my fingers and I hold them there while her climax takes her. She shakes all over, riding my fingers, and I know she cannot get enough as the orgasm seems to last forever.

As her body finally releases my fingers, I slide out and help her to the couch where she collapses against me, her breathing ragged. I wrap my arms around her, but every part of me is aroused, and I can barely wait for her to recover I want to fuck her so badly—this time with my favorite toy strapped to my body. Much, much harder and faster. She lifts her head to nuzzle my neck. "No ones ever done that to me," she whispers, and I smile.

"I know," I reply. This is only the beginning.

15

I listen as Claire's breathing returns to normal, and for a moment, I think she has fallen asleep. A smile plays over my lips, knowing I've made her come twice in a short amount of time, so her need for rest is expected. Only the smallest hint of disappointment makes me sigh. There will be time for more later. Lots of time.

"What are you thinking?" I hear her ask where she rests against me. I can't see her face, but her voice does not sound sleepy at all. Instead, it is slightly husky. Raising an eyebrow at this unexpected turn of events, I sweep a finger through the hair at her temple and tuck it behind an ear.

"I thought you were asleep," I respond and this makes her sit up and turn toward me. Her eyes lock with mine. There is a serious, sexy look there.

"Trust me, I'm not thinking about sleeping right now," she says and slides her hands up my body, reaching for the top button on my shirt. "You keep making me feel like that, and I promise I won't be going to sleep. Not until I give you something back." I suck in my breath at her words, and a burn of excitement runs down me as her fingers move to the next button. "But you need to help me." She tosses her head with a nervous laugh causing her long hair to cascade to the side. She looks incredibly sexy, but I don't interrupt her or try to take over. This is all her. "Because once again, I have no idea what I am doing."

She's on the fourth button, revealing the sports bra underneath. "You're doing great so far," I encourage and finally my shirt is unbuttoned, and she is pulling the hem free of my pants.

"How about we start by taking this off?" she asks, a hint of playful mixing in with the sultry while she runs a hand over my bra, grazing the tips of my nipples showing hard through the fabric.

"We can," I say with a smile as I slip out of my shirt, and then pull the sports bra over my head. As soon as it is free, Claire moves closer and kisses me. Her mouth is hungry on mine, but before I can do much in response, she moves to my neck. I lie back again, waiting to see what she will do next, and I am not disappointed as she continues to move her mouth over my skin. Her breath is hot on me, and I shiver with excitement watching her move to take my hard nipple in her mouth. Tentatively at first, it is sweet torture from the gentleness of the hesitant touch, but when I gasp, she gains confidence.

Pulling me into her mouth, she teases by flicking her tongue over the rigidness she seems to enjoy finding there. "Christ," I growl, and she smiles while nipping at me with her teeth. I buck in response. She's killing me, and it feels so good to know I am her first. "I'm going to make you pay for teasing me." Claire's answer is a long, hard suck on the nipple before she slides her body down mine while trailing kisses along the naked flesh of my stomach. The sensation of her full lips on me makes me shiver. This moment is incredibly erotic, and I cannot stop squirming.

She smiles again at my response. "You like what I am doing?"

"I do."

Moving down further, her hands slide to my belt, and anticipation makes me grit my teeth. Claire's slow seduction tests my every restraint. With a tug, the buckle opens, and she snakes the thing free of my hips before dropping it to the floor. Again, the simplest of these movements almost overwhelms me. The removing of my belt alone makes me wet. "May I unbutton your pants?" she asks, and I like this very much. As assertive as she is being, she remembers I am in charge after all.

"Yes," I reply, and her slow torture continues as she unfastens the button and takes down the zipper. Her lips graze the skin she finds just above my briefs. I can't suppress a moan and tip my head back.

"Is this okay?" she breathes.

"Very okay." I sense her appreciation of my encouragement, and in response, she reaches inside my waistband to tug down my pants. I reach down to help her and, in a moment, I am free of everything and am naked on the couch for her. Her eyes skim my body, and there is a mixture of appreciation, but also nervousness. "Only do this if you really want to," I whisper. She looks at me, and our gaze holds.

"I want you," she says, her voice low and full of desire. All I do is nod, waiting to see what she will do next and when she runs her hands up my thighs, the feel of it is so intense it almost burns me. I nearly lose my restraint. Flipping her over and fucking her is a craving I can barely resist. Biting my lip, I slow my breathing. Strangely, I suddenly feel like this is my first time too, and the ache in my body is not just between my legs, but also in my heart. That can't happen, and I start to sit up, needing to change our positions, but then she kisses the inside of my thigh, letting her tongue caress me, and I am overwhelmed with wanting to feel her mouth on me.

It is slow torture as she navigates higher up my thigh until she is poised just over my sex, and I tremble in anticipation. I am rewarded by the slow, cautious feel of her tongue dipping between my swollen lips. As she brushes my clit, I gasp. A moan comes from her throat as she continues to explore, and I close my eyes, letting my senses all focus on what she is doing with her mouth.

I've had sex with countless women, often letting them go down on me as part of the foreplay before I fuck them senseless. This is different. My need to come is intense, but there is an exquisiteness in her touch, and I want it to last. Perhaps forever.

"Is this okay?" I hear her ask, breathless.

"Yes," I whisper. "Don't stop."

She doesn't and begins to move faster, with more confidence. Her mouth covers my clit, and she sucks on me while I try to hold still. It is impossible, and I thrust my hips against her mouth, wanting her and unable to contain myself. To keep contact, she slips an arm around my thighs and holds me against her as she licks her tongue back and forth over my clit. The intensity makes me growl low in my throat. I need more. "Touch me," I demand, but the sound to my ears is more like a plea. What is happening to me? I can't let go. Not like this, yet something inside me wants to give myself to her. Only to her.

I don't know what to expect next, knowing she is a virgin at this, but I am rewarded with the feel of her hand sliding along my thigh and then her finger moving inside me. I am incredibly tight, and the sensation of being filled makes me cry out. Her mouth is back on my clit while she very slowly moves her hand back and forth, drawing me out. The touch of her inside me, something I rarely want, makes me feel so vulnerable and desired, I can hardly breathe. "Claire," I choke out. "Oh, God, who are you?" The tables have turned. She is about to make me come harder than I have in a long time. I quicken the pace of my hips thrusting, and she responds in kind, fucking me faster. Grabbing out with my hand, I take a handful of her long hair, almost desperate to find some sense of control again. Then, it doesn't matter, and the wave of my orgasm starts to overwhelm me. I fear for a second I will drown in it, but then the feeling of complete release crashes over me. I shake my head from side to side and hear someone whimpering. I know it is from my own throat, which is impossible. I never give in like this. Never.

Only when I stop shaking do I feel her pull away from me and crawl up my body to take me in her arms. There are no words to say, so she kisses me. Unlike the heat from our earlier embraces, there is tenderness. She has captured me. Somehow, when I wasn't paying attention, she found a way in. As I let sleep pull at me, I don't know what I will do about it.

16

A warmth throughout my body is what wakes me, I think. A sense of comfort and closeness I am not familiar with, and my instinct is to embrace it. To actually cuddle into the feeling, but then my sensibilities take over, and I open my eyes. I realize I am in the living room, still on the broad couch. The place is in shadows, but I have a sense it is almost morning. The sun will dawn just over the Chicago skyline any moment, and I consider getting up to watch it from the windows. I love the beauty of the start of a new day. Still, this is not why I feel so good. I realize we are under a sheet, and Claire is sprawled across my chest, her blonde hair fanned out, hiding part of her sleeping face. She looks lovely in her repose, and I don't want to disturb her. I also don't want to wake her for my own reason. Having her there, tucked in next to me, feels fantastic.

I am not a cuddler or at least not until now apparently. Women do not spend the night, and I do not spoon. Physical contact for me has the most basic agenda. The needs and desires of sex. Yet, here I am, holding Claire as she holds me, and I am happier than I can remember. Our night of love-making was exquisite, although simple. No strap-ons or silk ties to playfully restrain her. Just us, loving each other's bodies. That reality is hard to accept, and yet, I can't deny it was perfect. Claire is everything I could want and more. Sensual, willing, but also at rare times feisty. The future ahead looks bright, and I smile.

"I see you smiling," Claire whispers and I notice she is awake and looking at me. Her blue eyes are soft with sleepiness, which only makes me find them more appealing. Without thinking, I kiss her forehead, only to realize that is also something I've never done before. What is coming over me, I do not know. It's this woman. It's Claire.

"I'm smiling because I'm happy," I admit and this time kiss her mouth. When she parts her lips to allow me access to her mouth, I take it and the fire from last night immediately rekindles. I cannot get enough of her. Pulling back, I see the sleepiness in her eyes has been replaced with a passion of her own, and I slide my hand across her lower back. My reward is a gasp. "I want you."

"I want you too," she says, but before I can act any further my phone rings. I would normally disregard it, but it is making the chirp of a call from someone in the club. I must answer it.

I kiss her quickly again, before sliding out from under her. "I am sorry, truly, but I need to answer this."

"Of course," she answers and sits up pulling the sheet around her.

I walk naked to the phone and answer it while moving toward the bedroom to grab a robe, and also to keep the conversation semiprivate. "This is Madison." I'm not sure who I expected, but Val's accented voice snaps through the phone.

"What are you doing? Is this some kind of joke?" she

asks, although I can tell her words are not really a question, but an angry statement.

Frowning, I'm not a big fan of her tone. "I don't know what you're talking about?"

"Then I suggest you get online. You and some blonde are all over social media," Val says. I don't respond but instead, flip to an entertainment app on my phone. Val is telling the truth. A picture of Claire and I, grainy but still clear enough to tell it is me, is the headline. Someone at the baseball game recognized me apparently and snapped a photo with their phone. The two of us are locked in a kiss. The only good news is you can't really see Claire's face, and as I skim the short article, they refer to her as my mystery woman. "Fuck," I mutter and put the phone back to my ear. "I can't stay on. I need to deal with this."

"Pretty sure that's not going to be good enough," Val says. "Zena and some of the others have had enough. Not like we didn't warn you."

My chest tightens with anxiety. "What does that mean?" I snarl. I'm about done with the club trying to run my private life.

"We are calling a special meeting. Tomorrow. 9 AM. Hong Kong. You know the place."

A special meeting to discuss kicking my ass out. I feel it, and now I am furious. "Listen, it was you and the others idea for me to find some nobody and seduce her into settling down, remember? Not mine. All due to Zena and the fucking bet." I hear a noise behind me and glance to see Claire standing in the doorway. She holds a coffee mug in her hand, clearly meant to share. Her face is flushed, and I know she heard my last statement. Without another word to Val, I hang up and turn to her. "Claire—" I start, but she shakes her head to stop me.

"Don't," she says. "It doesn't matter. I'll just get dressed and go." Without another word, she retreats, and I quickly follow her into the living room. This is the last thing I want, and I toss the phone aside as I move toward her. She holds up a hand warding me off. "I mean it. But at least explain to me who you are." With a sigh, I tell her and watch as her eyes widen. I see she knows me by reputation rather than by my face. "I can't believe this," she says more to herself than to me. "This fucks up everything." There is a hint of tears, but she turns her head to look away from me before they fall. "And I was just a plaything."

"Claire," I start again, trying to keep the hint of panic from my voice, but she ignores me and goes into the bathroom. I pause before following her. I need to get my head on straight. I hurt Claire and feel sick about it. Resolving to make her listen, I go to the bath's doorway and find her in the middle of putting back on her clothes from the night before. I realize she has nothing else, and if she is spotted walking out of the hotel wearing the same things as the photo, her reputation will be even more tarnished. "Let me give you some clothes of mine."

"No," she snaps, the hurt in her voice making my stomach clench. "I can handle the walk of shame just fine, thanks. My first time so should be fun." The words are too much, and I move to take her in my arms, but she yanks her body away.

"Do not touch me."

I pull my hands back. "I'll call you a ride, at least. I insist. I can get you out undetected." I mean this. There is a way at my disposal.

She hesitates but then nods. "All right," she says. "But I don't want anything else from you. Ever."

I swallow hard trying to keep the strange lump in my

throat from choking me. I want to make her understand my words were in anger at the club, and not intended for her to hear. They were mean and hurtful, although true at their core, but I did not mean how it sounded. Claire is important to me. We are incredibly good together, and I can't let it end. "I want you to come back and sit on the couch with me and let me explain," I nearly beg.

"No," she says sliding her Cubs T-shirt over her head. As she pulls her hair back, combing it with her fingers, I am captivated by the sexiness of the gesture. Even angry at me, she is beautiful. "And I want my hat. It's important to me."

I nod. "Of course," I say. "We can find it. Are you sure—"

"Stop," she says pushing past me as she leaves the bathroom, but I hear the sob in her voice. "I want to go."

Frustration mounting, I know my time is limited. I need to organize transportation to Hong Kong and leave immediately if I hope to make the meeting. Being late will not help my situation. "Okay," I answer and go back to my phone. Tapping one button, I connect to my team. "Send Elvis One."

Claire watches me as I hang up. "What is that? Elvis One?"

I sigh guessing my choice will not sit well with her under the circumstances and the revelation of who I am and why she is here, but there is no better alternative. "It's my helicopter. To take you home."

*M*y pounding headache is not helped by the 'futuristic vibe' of the music in the Hong Kong nightclub. I am forced to push my way through the overly crowded space to get to the obscure elevator, which will descend to the secret basement conference room. Gyrating bodies and flirty looks do not help my mood either. I've traveled fifteen hours getting here, spending most of it with my emotions swinging from anger at being summoned, to worry over what will happen with Claire, to confusion about what I am feeling at all. My text messages to Claire have gone unanswered. The last I know of anything, was her drop off in the parking lot at her apartment complex. If I wasn't stuck here, doing this, I could go find her and insist she listens to me. I need to explain, and yet I am not even sure what I would say. That I don't want to be without her in my life? That I love her? I shake my head in frustration and then wince at the pain. Love is not in my vocabulary.

Before I make any more sense of it, I am at my destination. The elevator doors slide open, and I step out into a space as opposite from the nightclub above as possible. The techno lights and rainbow of colors have been replaced with the tasteful muted tones of dark wood accented with soft grays. A pair of Asian men in black suits stand in the foyer. They might as well have bodyguard stamped on their foreheads, but I get it. The city's underworld is not to be taken for granted. Kidnapping a room full of billionaires, not to mention lesbian ones, is enough to tempt more than one triad. All the more reason to keep this meeting short, and then I can be back on my jet out of here.

The bodyguards know me, but I am still asked to go through a retinal scan recognition. Again, we cannot be too careful. Finally, the double doors to the inner sanctum open, and I walk in to see a half dozen unhappy lesbians around a glass and chrome conference table. All are seated but the hostess, Yuki. This is her building, one of many. The room goes silent as I stop and take in the lot of them. Zena, Val, and thankfully Lila are there, as are three others I have not seen in a while. I swallow hard. This is even more serious than I thought if so many of us have answered the call. Kris, the other American in our billionaire group, a software technology magnate, is the first to look away and clear her throat. This is no surprise. I have not met a more socially awkward rich person anywhere. Because I am angry, her show of weakness draws my fire. "Hello, Kris," I snarl. "Come for the crucifixion?"

"Be nice," Zena snaps in Kris' defense. Her voice is cold, and I have had enough of the woman. This is all her fault. If not for her bet and subsequent ultimatum, I wouldn't be preparing to defend my personal life. To defend Claire. And my chest would not feel like someone was tearing a hole through it.

"Let's get this over with," I say, tired and hurting from

the headache, or at least that is all I am willing to admit hurts. I don't want to explore the rest right now. "Why are we here?"

The woman at the far end of the table, swiveling casually in the highbacked leather chair, snorts a laugh. "I think that's pretty obvious," she says, her accent smooth, her overall demeanor charismatic. Chloe. Australian. A close friend usually, but the derision in her tone makes me bristle.

"Explain it to me anyway," I say through clenched teeth.

Yuki walks over to meet me and offers a drink. Neat scotch and I am grateful. The petite woman, the picture of her culture's best attributes, nods when I accept it and take a long swallow. "Please, find a seat, Madison," she says with a wave toward the table. Lila sits to the left with an empty chair beside her, and I go to her as if she is a life raft. The sad smile she greets me with nearly does me in. I cannot believe they are really going to exile me over this. I sink into the chair and wait. My anger is starting to dissipate. Perhaps this group was never the right fit anyway. I am not good at following other people's rules.

Again, the group is silent, as if no one wants to be the bad guy, but leave it to Zena to step into the vacuum. "Who is the girl?" she asks. I lift my chin, ready to defend Claire and my decision to court her to the death. Zena and the others can go fuck themselves.

"Claire Hathaway. No entertainment connection. She didn't even know who I was until all of this." A couple members of the group nod, Yuki in particular, and I feel a spark of confidence that I can sway them. "If you let me, I believe she can be the one to 'settle me' as you previously insisted. Assuming she speaks to me again."

Chloe leans forward in the chair and puts her elbows on the table. "Have you lost her already? The great Lesbian-

Romeo? Isn't that what the tabloids call you?" she grins softening her questions, almost as if she's teasing me. I furrow my brow. If I'm in so much trouble, I don't understand why others are shaking their head as if amused by Chloe's statement. My irritation returns.

"Why is this funny?" I snap.

Zena raises her hand to refocus the group. "Madison, I'm sorry. I lured you here with a ruse about this being because of your indiscreet photo," she starts. "I'm not a big fan of how you're handling your part of the bargain necessarily. The idea is to get out of the spotlight, but I am sure you have a plan."

My mouth drops open I am so surprised. Val sighs and I look over at her. "Leave it to you to believe everything is about your life," she says. "But no, we have a much more serious problem."

Again, I am stunned. This is not about Claire and our affair after all. Perhaps a little, but clearly, this meeting has a different agenda. One I am yet to be privy to, and I look around at the faces of everyone else. I feel my chest loosen at the news. They are not kicking me out or asking me to abandon her. There is still a chance I can woo her back. As my brain races to catch up to the twist of events, I begin to see the bigger picture. Now things make more sense. Nearly the entire group has gathered on ridiculously short notice. "So, does everyone else know why we are really here?"

Zena nods. "Kris was just filling us in."

I raise an eyebrow. Kris having the floor is a twist. She rarely engages in conversation, although once drawn out is an interesting and charming personality. Then, a sick feeling starts to form in my stomach. If our tech member is explaining, I probably don't want to hear this. "Shit," I say. "Don't keep me guessing. What is it?"

Kris rubs her face and the tiredness there registers. "Approximately thirty-six hours ago, my Darknet contacts alerted me to an information breach on one of our members," she says, sounding technical as always. "A Dark Web faction we have yet to identify used the data to transfer money to an account my team has only this morning been able to trace."

I glance around the table. "Who's identity?"

Lila raises her hand. "Me."

I feel a hint of embarrassment when I realize her sad smile is not about my situation at all. She is in trouble, and all I did was think about me. I take her hand and hold it giving it a reassuring squeeze. "We can figure this out," I tell her. In fact, I am not as alarmed as I possibly should be. It seems tracking these crooks down is only a matter of time, especially if Kris has determined their account information, although cyber stuff is not my specialty. "How much money are we talking about?"

"Two hundred and seventy million," Zena says.

This gets my attention. I look hard at Kris. "But you know where it went, so can't you of all people, take it back?"

I hear a sigh from Chloe and glance over. "Pretty sure it's been liquidated," she explains. "The bastards are brilliant. They used the money to buy untraceable diamonds on the Dark Web."

"Oh, shit, that is a problem."

"Yes," Yuki agrees. "Especially since they have put out feelers for potential buyers already."

I sit back in my chair. Poor Lila. It won't be easy to hide this news from the world. Still, we are some of the richest and most clever women in the world. Zena clearly has gathered us here for a reason other than sharing horrible news. "So, what do we do?"

Zena gives me her small smile, and I suddenly feel like she has been handling me the entire time. "Good that you asked," she says. "You are going to buy them. We will back you the money, and you will be our front person."

Before I can even respond with a yes or no, the others are nodding. I see I have no choice, and since it is for Lila, I would have agreed regardless. All I do is nod.

Chloe claps her hands together. "Perfect," she says. "And after all, you do have a brand-new girlfriend. Surely she likes diamonds."

18

"We are one hour out of Chicago, ma'am," my private jet's copilot reports to me.

"Thank you, Walt," I respond with a sigh. "Please make sure there is a car waiting when we land."

"Absolutely." With a nod, he retreats to the cockpit. Indeed, this is good news to be almost back. I'm sick of being out of the loop. Even though I can run my vast business from the air, the craft is wired for every technological convenience, none of it helped me over the last fifteen hours. Claire is hiding, and nothing I try locates her. My team has been scrambling since I walked out of the conference room in Hong Kong and instructed them to take her flowers and provide her my phone number. No pressure other than a message I want to talk to her. Unfortunately, they took their eye off the ball and didn't track her for a few hours after dropping her off in Elvis One. Apparently, during that window, she vanished. It is incredible. Based on details given to me earlier by my investigator, I have my team discreetly checking on Claire's family and closest friends to see if she is staying with them. So far, nothing.

Frustrated, I press a number on the handset built into the armrest of my seat. My assistant answers before the end of the first ring. "Have you found her?" I ask before he even says a word. The nervous pause is evident even through the phone, and I grit my teeth. Clearly, the answer is no. "How is this fucking possible?"

"We have a flag on her credit and bank accounts," my assistant explains. "If she goes anywhere and tries to use a card, we will know instantly." I hate this. Guilt for invading her privacy nags at me, but I can't lose her. Not over this misunderstanding. Not over anything.

"Keep on it," I instruct making sure my disapproval resonates in my voice. "And tell me of any news immediately." I click off. There is nothing more to say. Claire does not want to be found, but I am not satisfied with that. She is making decisions based on partial bits of information. There is an explanation for what she overheard. I just need to tell her. When I find her.

Puffing out a frustrated breath, I contemplate ringing the flight attendant who is a permanent fixture on my plane. Like the entire crew, they are always on standby, in case I need to go in a moment's notice—such as an unplanned trip to Hong Kong. The plane is always stocked, and I could ask her to bring me another scotch. I consider this but then decide not to do it. I've had one within the last hour, and I want to be laser-focused once we land, so I can run the search in person. This has gone on long enough.

"And when I do find her, I won't let her out of my sight again," I mutter, tapping the arms of the chair with my fingers, feeling restless. The image of tying Claire up comes to mind, and I pause. Although that would only be a short, albeit extremely pleasurable option, I know the last thing I want to do is make her a possession. She must always be her own person. The last couple of weeks have proven this. Still, nothing wrong with a night of silk scarves and maybe a blindfold. I shift in my chair at the picture. Claire. Naked. Trusting me with her arms tied at the wrist and stretched over her head. I have a perfect spot for this. My mansion in Pacific Palisades in southern California has eight bedrooms, one of which I know is decorated with an heirloom cast iron bed as the focal point. I smile, thinking how easy it will be to tie her to it.

There is no doubt in my mind Claire will want me to do this. No woman has felt more sexually compatible. Even though she is at times hesitant because of her lack of experience, the desire to please me is always there. As is mine to please her. A night of soft bondage would be no different. I close my eyes tipping my head back against the chair to relish the fantasy.

"Are you okay?" I ask in my vision of her on the bed. "Comfortable?" The position has lifted her small, but perfect breasts. The nipples are pebbled and making me hungry to taste them.

"Yes," she replies, her voice a little breathless. I know this is turning her on, probably more than she expected. There is something about being tied up that makes a person feel less inhibited. As if they can't control what happens, therefore must submit to anything.

"Shall I tie your legs?" I ask, and she licks her lips. "Or will you behave?"

Her eyes meet mine, and a glimmer of desire shines in them. "Tie them," she whispers and the sensation this evokes in me makes my entire body tense with arousal. She wants to be entirely mine tonight. Taking another navy-blue scarf, I tie one ankle before moving to the other. Now that she is almost completely restrained, I use a little more force than before when I spread her legs. She gasps, and I know from experience the sensation of having her sex suddenly so exposed is highly erotic. A glance and I see how wet she is by the glisten. I want her so badly, I ache.

"Still okay?" I ask with a smile, and she nods, her chest rising and falling rapidly. I could leave her like this, make her wait until she is desperate for my caress. Long for me to fuck her. Perhaps I'll take a shower or go make a drink for myself, but that would be hard on me too. I can barely control myself as it is when I look at her. I feel my body reacting, and soon I will need release. But first, her. I run my hands up her calves, to her knees, along her thighs. Her body bucks under my hands then, and I know she is close already, even without my touching her anywhere else. I wonder how far I have to go to get her to come.

Slowly, I lower my head and stop just above where her clit is aching. Gently, I blow my hot breath on her and am rewarded with a cry of surprised pleasure. "What are you doing?" she gasps and I chuckle. I can't help it. She is hyper-sensitive by now, and the heat of my breath was a tormenting caress.

I repeat it, and this time she lifts her hips, searching for my mouth. "Please," she begs in a trembling voice. "Please." I can't resist such a sincere plea, and I slide my hand higher until one finger has slipped inside her. This makes her cry out again, and when I lower my mouth to suck on her at the same time I push deeper, she is already going over. Beginning to fuck her, in and out, I draw out the climax I know she is feeling because her body clenches my finger with each throb of her orgasm.

"Do you want more?" I ask as her body slows. This is just a tease. I plan to keep her tied up for quite a while. There is plenty I plan to do to her. She whimpers as I slowly pull out.

"I want more," she says so softly I almost can't hear it. "Don't stop."

I moan, loving that she wants what I want and slide my hand down—suddenly, I am interrupted by the chirping of the plane's phone system. With a growl, I open my eyes, letting the wisps of the fantasy slip away. I hate the disruption but pray it is news of Claire. "Tell me something good," I instruct the caller as soon as I press the button.

I am not reassured when my assistant clears his throat. "Ma'am, we think we have found Claire." Thank God, I think, relieved to have the search over as well as excited that I can perhaps continue my fantasy with Claire in the flesh. Soon.

"Please politely request her presence at the private terminal at the airport," I say. "Ideally, in the car." I know the approach is heavy-handed, but I can't wait to see her and begin to explain. To repair us.

There is a pause, and I frown, thinking my assistant is actually going to suggest a different approach to getting Claire back. The next sentence is the last thing I expect, but suddenly I know I was a fool not to suspect. "Corporate has been contacted by a man identifying himself as Johnny," my assistant explains. "He wants to speak with you. The message indicates he has something you will want."

My blood runs cold at the thought of Claire in Johnny's control. Then, it turns hot as I imagine the wrath I will rain down on the slimy son of a bitch from The Golden Rail. "I see," I say. "I assume there is a way I can contact him?"

"Yes, ma'am. A phone number. We have already determined it goes to a burner. Untraceable." Of course, I think, the man's a thug but not necessarily entirely stupid, aside from the fact he is messing with me. With Claire.

19

*M*y phone rests in my hand as I stand at the penthouse windows and look out over the great lake which borders Chicago. The sun is setting, throwing long shadows from the many skyscrapers which make up the city's skyline. I can't actually see the sunset, of course, as the lake is to the east and hence, I am facing away from nature's magnificent display. This is just as well, because I am not ready to watch the day end. Not yet. Claire is still in danger, and I will not rest until she is in my arms again. I take a deep breath to steady myself, and then I lift the phone to my ear. "Connect me," I say to the team listening on the line. There is a series of clicks and then the pulse of ringing. In a moment, the low creature named Johnny will answer, and I can't wait to talk to the stupid fuck. He's actually Johnny Tultino, and I know so much about him, the man's head would spin. An absent dad, a shitty childhood, high school dropout, and a short stint in prison for stealing cars. None of it matters to me. All I care about right now is the fact he is harassing Claire.

The call connects. "This better be you," I hear Johnny

hiss. "Because I'm tired of being jerked around." His complaint is legitimate. My team gave him the runaround for hours, buying me time while I landed and set up a plan. Every resource I think I might need is on standby, including members of the club, to make sure nothing goes wrong with getting Claire back. I don't know what exactly the man wants yet, but it doesn't really matter, because I will meet it. For now.

"It's me," I reply. "Where is Claire?"

The bastard chuckles. "Is that all you're worried about? How sweet. You missing your new girlfriend?" he laughs. The sound makes my skin crawl, but I keep my voice light when I respond.

"I am," I admit. "Let me talk to her." The demand comes out more severe than I intend, and I hold my breath to hear his answer. For the moment, I do not want to antagonize him. Although I am confident he would never hurt Claire physically, he's too much of a coward to risk real trouble, I know this situation will upset her. My priority is getting her away from him, so I can fix this.

"In a minute," he says, and I relax when it is clear he is unphased by my tone. He's used to being talked down to, so my demand is nothing new. "First, let's talk business. I have something I think you want, all things considered."

I grit my teeth with impatience. "I assume you mean Claire." Again, he laughs and I long to reach through the phone to choke him with my hands but will play his game if it means getting this over with.

"Sure, her," he says, utterly dismissive of the one part in this I care about. Stupid fuck. "But that's not the real treat. You'll love this one."

I breathe in a deep breath and then out slowly letting a calm settle over me. Here comes the thing I am sure Claire has been hiding from me. Things start to make sense. Black-mail. "What is that?"

"Well, our friend here, she's been a very bad girl," he teases. "You like porn, superstar? A little fuck video?" I blink. The idea sounds preposterous. Claire is too smart to do something like what Johnny is claiming. Still, even if it is true, I would never judge her. We all have pasts. Each has made choices we later regret. Myself especially, and I choose to live for today.

"I see," I say my voice cold as ice. "And now you think you've won the lottery? Because if you leak it with Claire's identity, it will make me look bad. And embarrass Claire."

"Bingo!" he says, the smugness in his voice grates on my nerves. Johnny is so going to pay. "I must say, when I saw that photo of you two making out at the Cubs game, I about fell over. I mean, you? And sexy Claire?"

"Let me talk to her," I demand having heard enough. "And then I will wire you whatever amount you want for the video." It's bullshit, but he doesn't know it. I swear I hear him lick his lips at my response.

"No funny business?" he asks.

"None," I lie. "Give her the phone."

There is a pause, and then she is there. "I am so sorry for this," Claire says, a slight tremble in her voice. She is upset, but not crying, and I realize she is too strong to let Johnny win. I love this even more about her, and my heart fills with joy at the sound of her voice. My Claire.

"Everything will be okay," I reassure her. "But I need to know one thing."

"Anything," she whispers.

"Do you want to come here?"

She hesitates, and I feel a tremble of uncertainty pass through me. If my decision to not be honest with her from the beginning costs me this woman, I will never forgive myself. Finally, I hear her suck in a wavering breath. "Yes."

My heart starts to beat again. "Thank you," is all I say. She has no idea how happy she makes me. "Please hand the phone back to Johnny." I hear a rustling as the phone is transferred and then the blackmailer is back. I hear him breathing, so I continue without waiting for him to speak. "Whatever you want, I'll transfer half now. Half after Claire arrives here safe. You will delete all copies of the video. Any questions?"

"Don't you want to see it?" he asks sounding sincerely surprised.

"No, it holds no interest to me. Destroy it. Everywhere. Do we have a deal?"

"Deal," he says with glee in his voice. "I want—"

"Tell my team. They will take over this call. Send Claire to me. You have thirty minutes, or the deal is off."

He starts to reply, but I've had enough and drop the phone onto the couch. It's time for a scotch as the next half hour looks to be a long one.

And I am right. The time goes unbearably slow as I pace the rooms. My drink goes down too smoothly, and I move to make myself another when the doorbell chimes. I drop the glass onto the counter and in a few fast strides, am at the door. It seems impossible she is already here, and I try to temper my hopes but rip the door open anyway. My reward is the tear-streaked face of Claire. I open my arms, and she steps into them, suddenly making me feel a completeness I never knew existed. Pulling her against me, I hold her tight. "I am so sorry," she shakes against me, and I run a hand over her hair. Hearing her cry nearly breaks my heart.

"Claire," I murmur. "I'm the one who is sorry. I should have told you everything from the beginning."

She pulls back and looks into my face, taking it in her hands, and I nearly melt at the feel of her touching me. "I need to explain about the video." Taking a deep breath, she plunges on. "My ex-husband, he taped me... I didn't know it was happening. Then he sold it to Johnny." A fury unfurls in me at this new information, but I lean into her, kissing her, trying to focus on just her right at this moment.

"I don't care," I say meaning it. Nothing Claire did in the past matters to me. Nothing. Any mistakes are forgiven. I only want her as she is today. "I really do not. Is this what you were afraid I would find out?"

She nods, and I pull her against me. "I don't care," I repeat.

She buries her face in my neck, and I feel the wet tears on her cheeks, but her crying has stopped. She believes me, I feel it. "But he wants a lot of money," she mumbles. "And I don't believe that he will actually delete it. That is why I could never get out of it." She lifts her head. "I need you to know I am not afraid of the video, but my brother and my mom. They would be hurt by it."

I run a hand down her back, wanting to soothe her. "It will be okay," I promise her with a smile. "Please trust me." She might know who I am, but she clearly does not realize what that means in the grander sense. "Will you be okay for a second? While I get my phone?"

Claire nods, and I step away just long enough to grab it off the couch. I press the app to call members of the club. Kris answers in one ring. I imagine her surrounded by computers and monitors in her high-tech fortress of solitude. "I'm listening," she says, and I appreciate her efficiency.

"It's a video," I say. "Sex. Made without her knowledge or consent."

I hear Kris puff out an angry breath. This is precisely the kind of things she hates, and I know it. Too much technology is used against women and children. "Your team sent me the information on the blackmailer," she says. "A complete wipe?"

I look over at Claire, who watches me. The worry still in her eyes is all the motivation I need. "Yes. Everything he has ever touched. Erase it. Make it as if he never existed."

20

$\mathcal{I}$ disconnect the call and see Claire staring at me. Our eyes meet, and I cannot read her expression, which surprises me. Usually, people are an open book as far as I'm concerned, but no, not Claire. She is complex—much more than people realize. The tears are gone, and she has gathered herself looking thoughtful and serious. I'm not sure what to expect. Of course, not gratitude, as what I have just done to our blackmailer was for my own protection as much as hers. Perhaps for a fleeting moment, I think she will be impressed, but again, that is not something I care about or the point behind things I do. Ever. Finally, she tilts her head and steps closer. "Then, it's finished? The video of me is gone?"

I nod. "Yes, my colleague will ensure no trace of the thing exists anywhere. Even if Johnny has a physical copy on a flash drive, if he tries to access the internet at any time, he will be flagged as a hacker. The data will be considered a virus and blocked. Forever."

Claire shakes her head, relief and a little incredulity on her face, as she looks away at the windows which are now showcasing a twilight sky over the city. "So, it's finally over," she says more to herself than to me. I wait as she processes this. After another minute, she turns back, and her face is softer. "I don't know how to thank you."

"That's not necessary," I say, although a part of me can think of ways she could easily thank me. The sexual energy between us, even at this moment, is still there. The chemistry. The passion. A small flutter of desire tightens my stomach, but I ignore it. This is not the time. She is still dealing with everything, I can tell. Plus, there is the fact I lied to her by omitting who I am, what I represent, which will need to be reconciled. "You don't owe me anything." It is my turn to look away as I stare at the floor and take a deep breath before continuing with the last thing I ever want to say to her. "You can go if you wish. I only brought you here to ensure you are safe. It's up to you."

There is silence between us, and I don't meet her eye. As unusual as it is for me to be afraid of anything, I actually fear if I look, I will see her answer is to leave me and in doing so, leave me devastated. Then, I hear footsteps and can't stand that she is going. She at least needs to listen to me and let me explain things. "Claire, wait," I start, looking up to see she walked toward me and is only a foot away. So much emotion is in her eyes, and I see a war going on there. It is easy to guess her conflict, and I hate myself for making her feel any of it.

"I'll stay," she tells me. "For now. But you hurt me."

"I'm sorry," I tell her, a phrase I don't use often, but this is heartfelt. "I should never have deceived you. But I had reasons."

Claire regards me, not responding. I swallow, not used to this kind of scrutiny in my regular life. I am always the one in control. People answer to me, not vice versa. "And the bet?" she finally asks.

At this, I sigh. The stupid bet. "Between a friend and myself. Over sports, which I lost. The penalty, if we must call it that, was for me to stop making headlines."

She furrows her brow. "Headlines? How does that pertain to me?" she asks.

I reach out my hand to take hers. "Can we sit? I will explain what I can, but it's complicated. My friends are very private." She ignores my gesture but sits on the couch. I join her, getting as close as I dare, and wait for her to look at me again. After a moment, she does, and I see less anger and more confusion. "My friends, who are also lesbians, need me to stop making headlines by being seen with so many different women. Stop being so public about it. They want me to find someone and stick with her," I say realizing how shallow and ridiculous it must all sound.

"And you picked me?" she asks, the anger flashing in her eyes and I reach out again, this time taking her hand before she resists. I slide closer and our knees touch. My body has longed for this contact, more than I realized, but I stifle my desire to do more, even though I want to kiss her so bad I ache for it.

"You hit me with your car," I answer with a smile. "And when I opened my eyes, there you were. I can't explain what happened next other than I was captivated by you instantly." Putting my other hand over hers, I slide closer still and our thighs touch. A hint of color rises to Claire's cheeks, and I know she is feeling the power of the electricity between us too. Encouraged, I charge on before I lose my nerve. "I have a confession."

Her eyes hold mine. "What is it?"

I pause, knowing what I am about to say is crazy and

might scare her away, but I need to tell her. "Since that moment, when I first saw you, you are all I think about. Day and night. Always."

In response, she leans into me until our faces are close and never in my life have I wanted to kiss a woman more than at this moment, but I wait. I need to know her response first. Finally, she whispers her answer. "You are all I have thought about too," she says, so close I feel her breath on my lips. "All of the time. I crave you." Then, she kisses me, and the kiss sears me, the heat of it is so intense. As she parts her lips to invite me in, I take her mouth with my tongue. A moan escapes her throat, and I slide closer, putting my arms around her waist to pull her to me. My passion for her pulses through my body and the hunger is strong. I could push her down on the couch and ravish her in an instant, but before I can, her hands are on my chest, stopping me. "And the bet?" she asks making me pause.

"It's over," I tell her because it is true. If Claire wants to leave and never see me again, I will not look for another woman to take her place. I will settle down on my own, stop making headlines, so the club is pacified, but no one else can replace her. I only want Claire, and as crazy as it sounds, I believe she is my destiny. I feel it, and there is no choice in my mind other than to wait for her as long as time exists. "I want you for you, no other motivation. No other reason."

Claire looks hard into my eyes, and I know she is reading them for truth. For her, I let my guard down so she can see the real me and know my heart is sincere. "I believe you," she says after a pause and stands suddenly catching me off guard. For a second, I think she is leaving. My heart races at the thought, but then she walks toward the penthouse's main bathroom. "May I take a shower? I need one after being cooped up with Johnny for two days."

"Did he hurt you?" I ask the fury from before flashing back. It is replaced with relief when she shakes her head and starts across the room.

"No, he wouldn't dare," she says. "My brother would kill him if he touched me. Johnny's only power over me was the video." She pauses and looks out the windows again at the night. The city lights are starting to sparkle. "You know, that's the only reason I agreed to work at The Golden Rail. And now, thanks to you, it's done."

I stand up to join her, wanting to hold her again. "I promise, Johnny holds no power over you anymore."

She turns to me, raising her hand, and touches my face. The gesture is tender, and I cannot help but lean into the caress. I miss her. "Thank you," she says and kisses me gently. "I will never forget this." Then, she turns away and continues toward the bathroom. "But now, a shower." I nod trying to keep my composure when I think of her naked under the hot water. While I wait, I will make a drink and behave myself. As I watch her go, when she is almost to the door, she glances back over her shoulder at me. "Aren't you coming?"

21

The shower slowly fills with steam as I undress. Like the rest of the penthouse, the master bath is grand, and the luxurious walk-in shower is its centerpiece. Claire is already naked and under the spray of hot water, letting it cascade over her in a manner so sensual and erotic, I pause to watch. Her long blonde hair slowly turns darker as she wets it, and I have the sudden urge to take it in my hands. I quickly finish removing my clothes and join her just as she turns her back to the spray. Her body is on display for me and a throb of desire pulses between my legs, so intense I tremble. The heat of the water, and perhaps my proximity, has tightened her nipples and made her skin flush a pinker shade. I want all of it, but first, I am drawn to her hair.

Stepping closer, so our skin brushes, I feel her body stiffen with excitement. This dance is not just for me. I reach up and take a strand of her hair between my fingers, relishing the texture. "Let me wash this for you," I say looking into her eyes. There is so much passion there, so much want, I almost reconsider. Taking her in the shower at this moment is very appealing, but I also know anticipation is the greatest aphrodisiac. After a moment, she nods, making me smile. I am grateful she has come back to me, and this can be part of my apology.

Gently, I turn her around, relishing the feel of her under my hands. Hot, wet skin. So tempting, but I inhale a deep breath to calm my racing heart. The need to take her is strong, but I pick up the shampoo and put some in my hand. Slowly, I lather it in her hair, running my fingers through a little at a time, and appreciating the beauty of the color. Golden, my favorite, and long trailing down between her shoulders. So perfect. Massaging as I go, I hear her moan under my touch, and again I must check myself as I twitch in response. This is such sweet torture for both of us.

"Turn around," I tell her, and she obeys closing her eyes before tipping her head back so the water pours through it, rinsing away the soap. Some of it slips down the front of her, and I bite my lip when it slides over her hard nipples. This is too much to bear. I reach out to run my thumb across her breast's surface. If I surprise her, she doesn't show it and instead arches into my touch. I growl in response as my fingers slide over her slippery skin and squeeze. She shivers but keeps her eyes closed, pushing harder into my hand, and I love how she relishes my touch. Slowly, I step closer until we are pressed together under the hot spray. The mixture of the wet heat and the slide of our skin on skin is exquisite.

With her head back, I see the contour of her neck and the beat of a racing pulse. Moving on instinct, I run my tongue along the spot and am rewarded with a gasp. The sound drives me crazy, the way she does it, and I answer by trailing my mouth up her neck until I am at her ear. "I want you," I whisper, and her hands reach for me slipping around my waist.

"Then take me," she moans, and the words make me want her all the more. Never have I had a lover more in sync with my need. An ache between my legs threatens to distract me, yet, I want to go slow. I want to relish this moment a little longer because once I start to fuck her, I won't be able to control myself.

"Turn back around," I say, and she does so without question just before I take her by the hips to roughly pull her backside against me. Again, she gasps, and I bite my lip with anticipation. "Lean forward. Put your hands on the wall."

She does what I want, splaying her fingers over the gray tile, then looks over her shoulder at me. "Like this?" she asks, her voice breathless. I know she is as turned on as I am, and this thrills me as I move my thigh between hers to spread her legs. "Yes," I growl. "Perfect." Even in the steam of the shower, I feel the heat between her thighs on my skin. As I slide my hands up her back, wrapping one in her hair running down between her shoulders, she begins to tremble. I know she does not know what to expect, which excites her even more. A small smile plays over my lips, and I decide to tell her as I move my other hand down her body. "Claire, I'm going to take you from behind. Right here in the shower."

Her cry of anticipation is all I need to slip between her legs and find her swollen lips. They are spread and inviting me in. With a moan I can't control, I fill her with two fingers, while I hold her in place with my hand clenching her hair. She is trapped against the tile and my hand inside her, and I can tell by her moans, she loves it.

"Oh God," she cries when I pull out and then slide back in, harder and faster than the first thrust. "You feel so good."

"What do you want?" I ask her, and I thrust inside her again, going deeper. She whimpers and doesn't seem able to answer, so I pull back and wait. "Answer me. What do you want?"

"You," she moans. "I want you."

I reward her with another thrust with my fingers, and then another, going faster. "And how do you want me?"

A low moan comes from her throat. "I want you harder," she gasps. "Harder." I comply, bending her forward a little more by her hair before moving to three fingers and stretching her until she is full. Another cry from her mouth. "Jesus," she pants. "You're incredible." This is what I want to hear from her, need to hear from her, and I fuck her faster. She starts to buck her hips to match my thrusts, and I know she is close.

"Tell me when you come. Scream it." This is all she needs, and as I continue to slide in and out, the orgasm rocks her.

"I'm coming," she cries out. "Oh God. What are you doing to me?" It is all I need to nearly push me over as well, and I slip out of her to touch myself. My clit is throbbing, and with practiced fingers, I make myself climax while the waves of pleasure still wash over her.

Before the intensity subsides, I turn her around and take her in my arms. We both tremble on unsteady legs, so I just hold her for a minute letting the hot water rain down on our bodies. She nuzzles her face in my neck as her breathing slows toward normal. "How do you know just how to touch me?" she asks. The question is a good one. My body seems to know exactly what Claire needs without my really thinking about it.

"I don't know," I admit. "But I wouldn't change it."

"No, don't ever change it."

"Never," I promise and reach past her to turn off the spray. "Come to bed. You need to sleep." She nods against my shoulder.

"I didn't sleep last night. Not while I was being watched by Johnny." The image of the man even slightly near Claire makes me clench my teeth with fury. For a moment, I wonder if erasing his identity digitally suffices, but then I feel Claire shiver.

"Let me get us towels," I tell her, and she pulls back enough to let me slip out to grab two giant white terry cloth bath towels. I take one and wrap it around her body to ward off the chill. The sudden memory of her photograph taken by my investigator and my fantasy over it comes to mind, and I can't believe how much has happened in such a short time. The intensity of my feelings for her makes me pause. It seems impossible to be so suddenly lovestruck, and yet, this is my reality. In an instant, she had me, and I don't want to ever go back to a world without her.

"What are you thinking?" she asks, taking the second towel from my hands and gently wrapping it around my shoulders. The answer is on the tip of my tongue. I want to admit I may be falling in love with her, but a part of me resists. The excuse she will think it's too soon comes to me, but that is not it. I know in my heart she is falling in love with me also. Only one thing stops me. Fear. As if the words 'I love you' will tempt fate and everything that is between us will be gone in the blink of an eye, never being real at all.

22

A kiss wakes me. Slow and sexy on my mouth, lips barely brushing mine, bringing me to consciousness with a wave of desire. I blink my eyes open to see Claire looking down at me. Our eyes meet, and she smiles as she slips her leg over my hip sitting up to straddle me. "Hi there," she says, and I drink in the sight of her. Her blonde hair, tousled from our shower sex, hangs over her shoulder. I see she found my shirt from the night before and is wearing it half unbuttoned with what I am pretty sure is nothing else. So erotic, and sleep leaves me. I am turned on in an instant.

"Hi there," I reply running my hands up her thighs to her hips. "I like your shirt." She laughs fingering one of the still fastened buttons.

"You do?"

I nod. "I do. But probably more if you take it off."

Her smile turns sultrier as she unfastens the one button and lets the shirt open wider. The curve of a breast draws my eye causing a pulse of excitement deep in my body. She moves lower and undoes another, this time pulling the shirt back to expose a swollen nipple. I reach for it, but she leans back away from my touch. "Not yet," she murmurs and my arousal surges. Dropping her hands to the last button, she pauses with half-closed eyes full of the same hunger as I feel. I wait clinging to only a thread of patience. "This one too?" she whispers.

I suck in a breath. "Yes," I answer hearing the huskiness in my voice. God, I want her. I already know there will never be a time I don't. She stirs something in me I cannot deny. Finally, the button is unfastened, and she is exposed for my pleasure. "You are so beautiful." She tilts her head running a hand through her hair, even more sexy in this unconscious gesture.

"So are you," she says taking my hand from her hip and placing it on her breast. I growl as she presses it against her and arches her back. "I want you." I feel her heart beating a rapid pulse and know what she tells me is true. This pleases me more than I could imagine, and just as I think our morning is going to be special, there is a buzz from the penthouse's front door.

I furrow my brow. No one should be at my door. The hotel is secured to keep this from happening. A look of surprise crosses Claire's face as well. "Ignore it," I tell her and try to recapture the moment, only to hear the buzz again. Longer and more insistent. Whoever is pressing it is going to pay for interrupting my morning, especially when Claire rolls off me.

"You should check," she says, and I know she is right. Hardly anyone knows I stay here, so it must be important. It had sure as hell better be. I roll out of bed, grab my robe, and stride toward the door. Not until I peek through the peephole do I pause. It's Chloe—the Australian lesbian from our club. She reaches for the buzzer again, but I yank the door open before she touches it.

"What in the hell are you doing here?" I ask. It is not particularly unusual for members to visit each other, but common courtesy dictates a phone call first.

"Room service!" Chloe says cheeky as always. I notice she carries a box of Chicago's famous Do-Rite donuts and shake my head.

"Seriously, what are you doing here?" I ask again. "This is not a great time." Thinking of Claire straddling me a moment ago, that is an understatement.

Chloe grins. "No time to waste, mate," she answers. "We need to talk. You need to go to Los Angeles. Tonight."

With a sigh, I step aside so she can enter. "Get in here." Chloe does, walking boldly across the room as if she owns the place. Only when she sees Claire standing in the bedroom doorway in a robe, does she pause. A glance back at me, and I see from her grin, she approves. Chloe might not make headlines as I do, but her 'appreciation' of beautiful women matches my own. Or at least it used to before I met Claire. No longer.

"Claire, I presume?" Chloe asks, and I nod.

"Claire, please meet one of my best friends, Chloe," I say. Since we don't use real names, the introduction is not a risk to the group.

"A pleasure. You are a lovely sight," Chloe says, a hint of flirtation in her voice. I don't take offense. This is simply Chloe's way, and I know it is meaningless. She would never truly make a pass. "Donut?"

Smiling, Claire walks to my side, leaning close as she puts a hand on my shoulder, and I slide my arm around her waist. I love the message she sends to Chloe—that she belongs to me. "The pleasure is mine," she says before turning to me. "Do you need me to go?"

I look to Chloe who shrugs. "I say we keep her in for this, but it's up to you. You're going to need a girl on your arm for the thing regardless."

Frowning, I consider her words. "And the risks?" Nothing will make me put Claire in danger, no matter how deep my loyalty to Lila and the others.

Chloe sets the donuts on the monster-sized coffee table and takes one before looking back at me. "Everything has risks, Madison," she answers and bites into the pastry. I feel Claire stiffen under my arm. Clearly, she is not happy with this reply, and I look at her. Before I can say anything, she lifts her chin, determination in her eyes.

"If you will be in danger, I want to help you," she says, and I understand any answer other than letting her come with me will not go well. "If nothing else, I owe you for helping me with Johnny." Her face softens. "But I also want you safe."

Our eyes hold, and a mixture of emotions run through me. Already, she is everything to me. The need to keep her safe is strong, but I also know we will be an unstoppable team. If I must have someone by my side for this, Claire is the only one I want it to be. Leaning in, I kiss her. Meaning to be tender, I cannot help but feel the passion behind it when our lips meet. This woman turns me on like no one ever has in my life. Chloe clears her throat. "Okay, lovebirds, we don't have all day. What's the verdict?"

Breaking the kiss, I smile at Claire for a moment, and she nods, understanding what I am about to say by instinct. We are that connected already. "We are in this together," I turn to my friend. "Tell us about the plan."

"Excellent," Chloe says, licking the last of the donut's frosting from her fingers. "We will have a conference call on your plane as you head back to the west coast for the small details, but I can give you the highlights."

I lead Claire to the couch, and we sit while Chloe takes the chair. She looks at ease as always even though I know the situation is stressful for her as well. One of our close-knit group is under attack, by an invisible, yet a hugely powerful threat. I don't need it spelled out to me to know this Dark Web faction could make any of us vulnerable. "So, talk," I say. "Then I'll arrange for my jet."

"Right," Chloe starts. "We've been in contact with the diamond sellers online and arranged for you..." She looks to Claire. "... and you to view the merchandise before buying." I frown, not liking the sound of this already.

"Where? Someplace with lots of visibility, I hope."

Chloe grins. "How about the Hollywood Gala? Getty Museum, day after tomorrow?" This is impressive. The gala is a huge evening event, and only the rich and famous will be in attendance. I have an invitation for two, of course. Zena and the others no doubt picked it for this reason. Still, the question is who the thief could be, and if he or she can arrange an invite as well.

"I will agree to that," I answer. "And assuming we are shown the diamonds somehow, then what?"

"You make the transaction," she says. "Payment of two-hundred seventy million in Bitcoin." If Claire is impressed by this number, she doesn't show it. Her demeanor, even in a robe with next to nothing on beneath it, is calm and, if I'm reading her right, a little calculating. Pleased, I take her hand.

"I assume we have a plan to recover those funds once I walk away with the inventory?"

"Naturally," Chloe says leaning forward to dig into the box for another donut. "You know, you really should try these. They are delicious."

23

*C*laire is asleep on the chaise lounge in the sitting area of my jet. As I sip my scotch, my eyes take her in. In repose, she is even more beautiful. The softness of her face makes me long to touch her cheek, a tender caress. Perhaps feeling my stare, her eyes flutter open, and when she sees me watching, smiles. "How long have I been asleep?" she asks, and I smile back.

"A few hours."

"I'm sorry," she says. "I don't know what happened." She stretches her arms above her head, in a move so sensual a flutter of excitement pulses low on my body. It never ceases to amaze me how quickly I become aroused by this woman. She isn't even trying to attract me, but everything she does makes me want her. I sip my drink to keep myself in check. Ravishing her on the lounger can wait.

"It's been a crazy couple of weeks. You needed to rest," I say, and it is true. Today alone was hectic. After learning more details from Chloe, arranging for the jet and organizing my own things, then going by Claire's so she could pack, everything was a rush. Thankfully, the flight is giving us both time to relax. "Let me order you something. What would you like?"

She sits up, running a hand through her hair, which I've come to realize is entirely innocent on her part, yet drives me crazy. I grit my teeth and wait for her answer. "A gin and tonic?"

I press the call button for the flight attendant and put in our order. A fresh scotch for me and Claire's choice. While we wait, I enjoy just sitting and looking at her. I feel like I could do it for hours. Saying nothing, just drinking her in with my eyes. I am completely captivated. She sees me watching and tilts her head. "What are you thinking?" There are so many answers to that simple question, I don't even know how to explain them to her. I am thinking I want her naked beneath me. I am thinking she makes me feel sexy and powerful. I am thinking she is everything I could ever want in a woman. Instead, I shrug.

"Just wondering what you thought of all of this? Now that you know," I finally reply. "It must seem a bit much."

Claire looks around the jet, a thoughtful expression on her face. She is surprisingly unphased by all of it, and I love that about her. She seems so capable of taking everything in stride. "I think somehow I knew you were someone special," she finally tells me. "Not a rich media giant, of course." She laughs, and I love the sound so much, I laugh with her. "But someone confident and powerful. I was entirely drawn to you from that first moment in the diner." She blushes. "And when you defended me, well, I was totally yours then."

"But you said no when I asked you to dinner?" I remind her. She sighs.

"You know now why I couldn't involve you in my life," she answers. "But I wish I told you everything from the first minute."

"I wish that too," I agree. "But here we are, and I wouldn't change anything just in case it ruins this."

She sighs. "I know. But can I be honest?" she asks.

I nod. "I want nothing else."

Claire looks away, the hint of color on her cheeks deepens. "I feel a little like Cinderella," she whispers. I love this answer. She truly is my Cinderella, and I could not be more grateful to have found her.

"That makes me happy," I tell her and she looks at me, a seriousness in her eyes, but before she comments, the flight attendant comes through the curtain with our drinks on a tray. I watch as she sets my scotch on the small table in front of me, then does the same with Claire's gin and tonic.

"Is there anything else you need, ma'am?" she asks, and I raise an eyebrow at Claire.

"Hungry?" I ask, only to be surprised at her look in response. My blushing Claire apparently is indeed hungry, but not for anything the flight attendant can bring us. Another flutter of excitement rolls through me. After all, in all the rushing around, there was no time to finish what we started this morning in the penthouse. "We are fine, thank you. I'll buzz for you if that changes."

As the attendant leaves, my eyes hold Claire's. For a moment, we do nothing, but when she bites her bottom lip, I know exactly what she is thinking. "Come here," I instruct her, and she slips from her chair to come sit on my lap. "Kiss me." Again, she complies, and her mouth is hot on mine fitting so perfectly. The sexual need I feel from her thrills me, and when she parts her lips inviting me in, I take her mouth with my tongue, a moan in my throat. In answer, she runs her hands up into my hair pulling me in tighter. I ravish her mouth with mine, hungry for her too, and as it goes on, I realize I could do nothing but kiss her like this for hours. The passion behind each taste of her mouth, her tongue, makes need rage within me, and a pulse starts between my legs. There is something so magical about her mouth on mine.

Breaking away with a gasp, Claire looks at me with eyes full of desire. "How the hell do you kiss like that?" she asks, and I chuckle.

"I was thinking the same about you."

"God, it's incredible," she says turning on my lap to straddle me in the chair. The memory of her doing something similar just this morning comes to mind, and I am immediately wet at the idea we can finish what we started. I long to touch her everywhere. "What are you thinking?" she asks clearly seeing my desire in my eyes.

"I am thinking about how badly you teased me this morning while you unbuttoned that shirt."

"Are you?" She laughs and glances at the curtain where the flight attendant disappeared.

Curious about what she is planning, I nod toward the front of the plane. "No one will come back here without my permission," I explain, and I am rewarded when she pulls her shirt over her head and drops it to the floor. Under it, she wears a gray-blue lace bra that cups her breasts perfectly. I suck in a breath, and she leans in closer until my mouth is an inch from her skin.

She runs a hand along the edge of the fabric. "Do you like this?" she asks. I definitely do and lick my lips not able to form words. Noticing my reaction, a smile plays over her mouth. "I've never worn it. I bought it with some others for my job at The Golden Rail, but that was short-lived." She lets her fingers wander over to the hint of a nipple poking against the lace and traces the outline. "Because you saved me."

My answer is to lean forward, running my tongue along the curve of her breasts. She moans and boldly reaches behind her back, unfastening the bra, letting it slip to the floor to join her shirt. I pause for a moment to appreciate the sight before me. Perfect breasts, tight nipples. "Thank you," I tell her.

"No, thank you," she responds running her hands along my shoulders, and she pulls my head down to nuzzle her. Loving this side of Claire, I reward her by taking one of her swollen nipples into my mouth and teasing it with my tongue, before giving the lightest bite. She flinches, but does not pull away, and instead grinds her hips down against me. Happy, I continue to tease her with my mouth, feeling how incredibly hard she is now, and graze my teeth across the tender tip. This time she moans and presses forward into my mouth tilting back her head.

I smile and whisper against her skin. "You like that?" I ask, and Claire gives a little laugh.

"I guess I do," she replies. "It seems I like everything you do to me." No answer could excite me more, and I return to caressing the pebbled skin, pulling her in deeper, sucking harder. Again, she moans, moving her hips in response to the erotic sensation of my mouth on her, feeling the electric charge I know is running through her body. Her hands are still in my hair, and my excitement continues to mount. Soon I will need my own release, but at this moment, I nip and tease her as she grinds down even harder against my lap.

"My God, I think you're going to make me come just by doing that," she gasps, and I know she's right as I slide my hand up her body to softly pinch and hold her other overly sensitive nipple. A cry comes from her throat, and as I roll the tight peak in my fingers, her entire body begins to shake.

She is so close, and I pinch and hold again, just hard enough to make her gasp. My tongue continues to circle her other nipple making her anticipate what she knows is coming. A whimper from her throat lets me know she is ready, and I bite her gently, making her body spasm with pleasure. She pulls my head against her and rides my lap as she comes with a cry of release. As I let go of her nipples, I savor feeling her body shake as the waves of climax roll over her. The sensation is exquisite and has me so turned on, I almost come with her.

Slowly, her body settles, and her uneven breath calms. She rests her forehead against me. "Are you okay?" I ask, and she nods.

"What are you doing to me?"

This makes me smile. "Everything."

She lets out a deep breath, then takes her hands from my hair and runs them over my face. "God, you are so sexy," she says and looks into my eyes. "I love everything you do to me." My response is to kiss her, and although she just came, the heat between us is still just as searing. After a moment, she breaks away with a gasp. "But what about you? I want to make you come too."

I smile knowing I could not wish for more. "Then, hand me my scotch," I answer. "And kneel between my legs, so I can show you what I like."

24

*A*s my driver whisks us along the California interstate to my primary residence in the Pacific Palisades, I feel myself relaxing into the leather seat. Los Angeles is my home turf, where I made a name for myself in the cutthroat world of entertainment and media, and where I built my empire. Tomorrow night I will have to face the thief who is trying to destroy one of my closest friends, but at this moment, everything feels right. Especially, because with me is a woman who is everything I could have ever imagined in a partner. We are electric together, and with each passing minute, I feel more connected to her. Without thinking, I reach for her hand and interlace our fingers, something I have not done with a girl since I was a teenager, yet it feels perfect. She looks over and smiles, squeezing my hand. In her eyes, I expect to see excitement at our new surroundings, or even just tenderness, but instead, there is apprehension. "Are you okay?" I ask her.

She laughs nervously. "I've never really been outside of Chicago," she admits. "I'm just taking it all in." Although I never want her to worry about anything, her news pleases me. I have so much to show her. Most people don't realize it, especially the tourists, but the City of Angels is a sprawling paradox. Some of the wealthiest and most creative people in the world thrive here, and yet some of the worst neighborhoods, and the gangs who rule them, are only miles away. Although I often travel all over the world, this city is forever my home, and I always return to it, to recharge and regroup.

"You'll love LA," I promise her, and she quickly glances away with a hint of what I think may be tears in her eyes. Something is definitely wrong, and a squeeze of anxiety tightens my chest. "Have I done something to upset you?"

Claire shakes her head but looks down at our joined hands. "You've been amazing," she starts. "It's just..." She trails off, and I furrow my brow.

"Just what?" I ask softly, worried somehow, I have spoiled things in my excitement to be back in Los Angeles.

She takes her hand from mine and wipes at her eyes, frustration evident in her movements. "Maybe I'm just being silly," she answers then turns her face to really look at me. The seriousness I noticed earlier on the plane is back. "What am I doing here? I'm a waitress from the wrong side of Chicago. You can do so much better."

Instinct has me unhooking my seatbelt and sliding across the backseat to take her face in my hands. I look deep into her eyes and hold them. "You are what I want," I say with emphasis. "No one has ever made me feel like you do. Do you understand?"

Claire nods. "I think so," she answers. "Because I feel the same. But let's be honest, things are a little out of balance here."

"It doesn't matter to me," I insist, but I know she is not one hundred percent convinced. I suddenly realize going to my multimillion-dollar eight-bedroom mansion in the hills is not going to make this better. As much as I want to show it to her, to take her to my bedroom and make love to her on the rug in front of the fireplace, the place is enormous, extravagant, and therefore I imagine overwhelming. No, I need to slow down. Even Cinderella had time to process everything after the clock struck midnight. Claire deserves the same consideration.

I know what to do and, after kissing Claire gently on the lips, press the intercom to speak to the driver. "Change of plans. Please turn around and take us to the marina."

"No, don't change what you need to do," Claire says. "Please don't let me mess up anything. If you promise you want me here."

I cannot believe how she doesn't know how much she already means to me. Our connection is so strong it takes my breath away. All the more reason to do something different. "This will be better for our first night in Los Angeles, you'll see."

Claire's eyes search my face before she nods. "Okay," she says. "I trust you. Always."

As the car navigates the busy evening traffic, I sit with my arm around her pulling her closer against me. She puts her head on my shoulder, and the next half hour is bliss. Even with no words, our closeness touches my heart, and I think I could sit with her forever, but we are arriving at the marina. As the car slows, Claire sits up, and I am happy to see a renewed sense of curiosity on her face as we go through the gate. "Where are we?" she asks, and I smile.

This is a special place for me, where I go when I need to clear my head of all the world's craziness. "Marina Del Rey. I have a sailboat moored here."

She turns to me, eyes wide. "You sail?"

"I do," I admit. "Not nearly enough, I'm afraid, but I try

to go out when I can. I thought it might be nice tonight though. If that's all right?" She nods, clearly excited as the car comes to the dock. "Then, let me show you around."

I look out the window to see my pride and joy. My Catalina 375 sailboat. Thirty-five feet of sleek beauty. It is like coming back to see an old friend. Beside me, I feel Claire looking out the car window too. "She's incredible."

"She is indeed," I say while opening the car door before the driver gets to it. "Come on, you'll love her, I just know it."

Claire joins me, and I lead her to my slip. "*Water's Edge*," she murmurs as she reads the ship's name scrawled across the back.

"Like it?"

She nods. "Perfect for you."

I grin like a proud parent and help her aboard. Everything is in its place and well-kept, which pleases me. My team has done a perfect job maintaining this part of my life too. I make a note to reward them, then take Claire's hand. "Come below. I want you to see this." We duck inside, and she stops at the bottom of the steps to stare for a moment. I try to see it through her eyes and cannot help but smile. Everything a person would ever need is here, but compact. Perhaps I love coming here because it is such an orderly and efficient space.

"Madison," Claire says, finally moving deeper inside and running her fingers along the gleaming teak wood table, then the back of the cream leather bench seat. "I absolutely love this." I let out the breath I didn't even know I was holding and step closer to her, wrapping my arms around her waist to pull her against me.

"I hoped you would. Shall we go for a late-night sail around the harbor? I want to show you the stars once we get out past the city lights."

Her eyes widen. "Can we? Do you have a crew?"

"Not necessary," I explain. "The *Water's Edge* is just small enough I can take her out solo. Unless I am racing her."

Claire laughs. "Of course, you race," she says and puts her arms around my neck before kissing me. Her lips on mine feel as perfect as always, and what may have been meant to be a tender thank you, quickly is more passionate. The thought of taking her to my cabin and undressing her crosses my mind, but if we want to go out tonight, I have to contain myself. Breaking the embrace with a bit of regret, I look into her eyes. There is so much affection in them, I pause. Something special is happening between us, and I have sudden doubts about taking her with me to the gala tomorrow. If anything should happen to her... "What are you thinking?" she asks, and I know I've been caught. She already knows me so well.

"About tomorrow night," I admit. "I'm worried for you."

Claire touches my face, running her thumb over my cheek. "And I'm worried for you," she says. "Please don't go without me."

I sigh but know I can't resist her. If she only knew the power she already holds over me. "Yes, we make a perfect team," I admit, and she smiles.

"Then let's not think about it right now." She gives me a peck on the lips and dances away. "Show me the stars."

Laughing, I can't help but adore her enthusiasm and know I made the right choice coming here. "I will, but first we need to make her ready. You can help."

"Can I?" she asks, a gleam of excitement in her eye. "Will you show me?"

"Always."

25

With my arm around Claire's shoulders, we sit together under a blanket on one of the wide cushioned seats in the open-air cockpit of the *Water's Edge*. We rest with our heads tipped back to gaze heavenward. The night sky is in full splendor with not a cloud anywhere, and the moon is only just waxing so does not yet overwhelm the light of the stars. The slow, rolling movement of the sailboat is soothing, and only the slightest breeze brings the scent of the nearby open sea across the gentler harbor. I hear Claire sigh. "Everything okay?" I ask softly.

"It's so okay." She snuggles in closer to me. "Thank you."

"For?"

"All of it. But maybe especially this."

I have to agree. Tonight has been paradise. Simple. Tender. Exactly what we needed after the craziness of Chicago and before whatever might happen tomorrow. Rather than reply with words, I take her chin in my hand and kiss her. There is instant heat between us, and I am reminded of the first time when I waited for her in the parking lot of the diner. Our kisses then were so intense I was dizzy from it, yet even now, after so many kisses since, her mouth still makes me weak. When she parts her lips welcoming me in, I tease her gently with my tongue. I try to convince myself I am in no hurry, that I want to move slow and make tonight last. Yet, when I feel the tip of her tongue touch mine, my hunger for her blooms hot. Unable to help myself, I take her mouth with enough passion to make her moan in response.

By the time she puts her arms around my neck to pull me in closer and deepen our kisses, I know it is either undress her here on this bench or lure her inside to take her to bed. The image of her laying naked across the quilts in my cabin helps me decide. "Come inside with me," I murmur against her lips, and she nods. We stand, and I follow her down the three steps to the salon only to pause on the last one. My expectation is for her to sleep in my cabin and let me make love to her, yet for the first time, I hesitate. There are two small cabins aboard, and perhaps I should not presume anything. The strangest sensation of consideration for her comes over me. Our chemistry has proven to make us inseparable when we are around each other, yet I can't be sure she always wants what I want.

Clearly feeling me hesitate, Claire turns back. "What is it?" she asks, and I clear my throat.

"There's two cabins," I offer. "You know, in case you want some privacy tonight." She blinks as if I have said something incomprehensible. Then a slow blush colors her cheeks.

"Do you want privacy?"

"God, no," I assure her, realizing the message I am inadvertently sending. "I want you with me. All the time. I only, well..." I look away from her face. "I didn't bring you here just to sleep with you. It's important you know that."

Suddenly, her hands are on my face lifting my gaze back

to her and our eyes hold. "I know," she says. "And yes, I do want privacy, but only for a few minutes." A sultry smile crosses her beautiful face, and she leans in until her lips are less than an inch from my ear. "Then, I want you to take me like only you can."

My heart skips a beat at her words, and I suck in a breath. "I can do that, I assure you."

"Point me to my cabin," she says picking up her overnight bag from the luggage she brought from Chicago. The rest of her things have been taken to my mansion, yet she was adamant this one stay with her. I was intrigued then and now am more so. Luckily, I have everything I need onboard for impromptu visits. Although Claire is not the first woman I have brought aboard, in my heart, I feel she might very well be the last. All others pale by comparison, and I wonder what that will mean for our future. It's too much to wrap my head around right now. Instead, I bow.

"Right this way," I say and move across the small space to open a door with a flourish.

She pecks me on the lips as she passes by to go inside. "And your cabin? So I can find you?"

I wave to another door only a few inches from hers. "I'll be right inside. Waiting," I smile. "Probably naked." She laughs.

"Just the way I like you," she teases back and then closes the door. I don't hesitate to keep my promise, and when she knocks on my cabin, I am nearly naked under the sheet. But not quite. Tonight, I have something special in mind and only hope she will want it too.

"Come in," I say, and the door opens enough to reveal Claire in an ice-blue lace babydoll chemise and nothing else. The sight takes my breath away, and I lick my lips, knowing she dressed this way to please me.

Seeing my look, she tilts her head. "Is this okay?" she asks, her tone sexy and teasing.

"You look incredible," I whisper. "Come here." The room is tiny, and the bed takes up almost all of it, so she is forced to crawl across the mattress to reach me. The sight of her on hands and knees sends an ache straight through me, and a throbbing starts between my legs. There are so many ways I want her, and I have a feeling I will never get enough.

As she reaches me and slips under the sheet to lie back, I barely contain myself. Only the desire to appreciate the sight of her holds me back for a moment before running my hands up and down her body. Under my gaze, her nipples tighten and her eyes half close with arousal, driving me past any restraint. I want her, and it takes all my reserve not to hurry.

I move closer and kiss her. All my pent-up need is behind it, and she rolls toward me putting her arms around my neck. I could so easily move on top of her, but patience is essential right now. Yet, when she presses her body against mine, I see her eyes widen. Rather than try to explain, I guide her hand to the shaft of my strap-on, and while her hand explores it, I watch her face. There is a hint of surprise, but it is quickly replaced with desire, and I know I guessed correctly. A sly smile crosses her face, and she arches her back while she still holds me in her hand. "Are you going to fuck me with this?" she whispers, and I could not ask for more in a partner. Nothing is beyond what Claire will do for me. Nothing.

I nod. "I am," I answer as I slide my hands along her legs to widen them before moving between her thighs. The reality that I am poised to enter Claire makes me tremble. Never have I wanted this more, yet I force myself to move slowly. For now. "Talk to me. Tell me what feels good."

As Claire runs her hands down my back dragging her fingertips lightly across my skin, I shiver with anticipation. "You on top of me feels good," she murmurs lifting her hips a little to show me she means it.

"Jesus," I growl. Normally, I can control myself, but she draws out the hunger in me, and I push up on my hands to look down on her. The sight is breathtaking, seeing her under me, with her hair fanned out on the pillow and desire making her eyes darker. As I watch, she bites her lip waiting for me, and my answer is to shift my hips to enter her only the slightest.

Her eyes widen with excitement. "Oh God," she gasps. "You feel so good." She lifts her hips to help take me in, and I reward her with a slow thrust. Her hands clench my back as she throws her head on the pillows while a small cry of pleasure escapes her. I pause, remembering how tight she is, letting her grow used to me before moving again. I run my mouth over her neck, and she moans at the mixture of sensations.

"Kiss me," I demand, and she does, her lips open and ready for me to ravish her with my tongue. As I take her with a deep kiss, I thrust again, harder and she bucks under me while moaning into my mouth. Starting a slow rhythm, I feel her spreading open for me, and she breaks the kiss to throw back her head again as her pleasure mounts. Under me, her body matches my movements, lifting her hips to allow me to slide deeper every time. Her hands grab at my skin, and she wraps her legs around me, pulling me to her whenever I rock back before each new thrust.

Her breathing is ragged, and I feel her body starting to shake under me. Increasing the speed of my movements, knowing she is close, I shift my body forward until the pressure of the strap-on presses back against my clit and tortures me perfectly. Every time I slide in, my own pleasure mounts, making my breaths come quicker, and my heart pound. "Don't come until I allow it," I order her moving even faster, pounding against her body relentlessly.

"Oh God," she cries. "Please let me come." I love the sound of her voice begging me, and I nearly come myself but not yet.

"Wait."

We move even faster, her hips rising and falling in perfect harmony with my own push. "Please—"

"Wait," I insist leaving no room for argument. I want her to explode. A whimpering comes from her throat, and her head whips back and forth on the pillow in her need for release. The sight of her wanting me so badly is too much, and I feel the onrush of my climax. A growl rises from me and waiting is soon not going to be an option.

"Wait, Claire."

"Oh God, please... please."

Then it is too much, and I can't hold back. "Come to me," I say, and now I'm doing the begging. This time her cry is a scream of release, and as my body throbs with my own orgasm, I keep up my rhythm, riding through each wave of pleasure for us both. Not until her shaking starts to subside do I slow and then stop to let her feel me inside her as the last pulses of her body fade away. "I want more of that," she smiles when we are spent, and as I slide out of her, she arches her back while sheer bliss shines on her face. "A lot more."

I laugh softly as I lower myself to her side, resting my head on her shoulder. She strokes my hair and sighs. Words are not necessary as we lay in each other's embrace. I feel her in my soul and somehow know she feels the same. We have something magical between us, and I will never let it go.

26

*A*t my estate, I consider having another drink as I stand at the edge of my turquoise blue infinity pool and contemplate the horizon of the Pacific Ocean in the distance. The view is stunning, as well as it should be for what I paid for it, but this place is my oasis away from the craziness of Los Angeles. Once owned by a short but distinguished list of old-school celebrity A-listers, the three-acre estate hides among rosewood trees to keep away tourists and paparazzi. The rambling mansion of archetypal Mediterranean sits at the center. There is more house here than I will ever need, in fact, I rarely use it even to entertain, but the privacy suits me. I still wonder what Claire truly thinks of all this. She was quiet when we went through the arched gates leading down the winding slope to the grand front doors of the main house. Once again, I worry if I overwhelmed her as she watched out the window while we approached and I even considered if I should take her to my smaller loft downtown. Then, she turned to me and smiled. "Not what I would have guessed," she admitted. "But I love it. So tranquil and private. I see why you picked it."

I smile now as I smiled then, and when I took her by the hand to show her some of my favorite places inside, she quickly relaxed. The place is luxurious, but still, it represents my tastes, which not surprisingly appear to match her own. This includes the pool, where she stared for a minute at the view before putting her arms around my shoulders and kissing me. "Somehow, it is all so you," she whispers against my lips. "I think that is why I love it so much." I feel a sense of relief as she kisses me again. The feeling of her lips on mine start a fire within me and only the fact I want her to have time to shop for a dress tonight keeps me from taking her upstairs to my suite of rooms.

Rodeo Drive is where Claire spent most of the afternoon, and why she is now inside getting ready, albeit without me. My offer to join her on the venture was "no." She wants to surprise me, and I like it. Her desire to please me only makes me want to please her in return. Tonight, will be no different. I know she will look incredible. Although, to be honest, she could wear anything and people will stop and stare. The woman is unconsciously sexy and beautiful, a rarity in LA, which people will no doubt notice. I smile knowing from years of media experience, the cameras will love her. And there will be cameras. Lots of them.

As much as I wish tonight was nothing but a normal date at the Getty Museum's celebrity gala, it is far from it. Not only because of our scheduled rendezvous with the thieves, but because this is her debut with the media. The mystery blonde making her first public appearance on my arm. My name is on the thirty-thousand dollar a ticket guest list so the media piranhas will be waiting. All I can do is try to prepare her by explaining what the red carpet will be like with the throngs of fans and flashbulbs everywhere.

Paparazzi calling our name, no doubt asking who Claire is and how we met.

I might have second thoughts except for the need to use her as a distraction. She is willing to be used this way. Back in Chicago, Chloe asked her point-blank if she would help cover for me when I slipped away to make the exchange. Claire didn't bat an eye at the request. "Anything to help her," was the answer. All I can do is hope she doesn't regret the decision when people are tripping over themselves trying to know everything about her. Even with all the other big names who will be in attendance, Claire is about to be a celebrity overnight. Her face will be everywhere, at least temporarily as the long-term plan is to come back to my estate and hide until the frenzy dies down. Just as the members of the club requested. Even though I was bitter at the time, I am very much looking forward to time alone with Claire. Oh, the things we will do.

The plan itself, to exchange Bitcoin for diamonds, sounds simple. After dinner and the entertainment, I am supposed to peruse the art in the gallery. Eventually, I will make my way to the famous painting "Irises" and wait to be contacted. There is no code word apparently, which makes the whole cloak and dagger act seem somehow lacking, but I am not making the rules. Wondering who the thief might be continues to puzzle me. This is no ordinary event. Even if a person is willing to pay for a ticket, the gala is by invitation only. My only real guess is the Dark Web faction behind the theft is using someone else's identity. As they took Lila's, they would undoubtedly think nothing of taking on the persona of anyone else. To be honest, I am looking forward to meeting whomever they are face-to-face so I can see my adversary and quite possibly spit in their face.

Regardless, I am somehow supposed to scope the

diamonds, which I assume will be done in a private room and then provide the secure account number to a Bitcoin wallet containing payment. This is where the plan becomes tricky, and I must rely on Kris and the others to ensure the rest of the events go smoothly. If not, well, I will be in hot water. Before I dwell on it, there is movement to my right. I turn to watch Claire come out the French doors to join me poolside. The sight of her makes me catch my breath.

Every part of her is sensual, sexy elegance. I wondered while she was gone what her idea of the perfect dress for the gala might be. She asked no questions, and since it's everything goes as far as glamourous clothing designs at the event, I had no concerns she would look or feel out of place. This dress though—I am speechless and can only stare, I am so pleased. Jet black. Sophisticated scoop neck. Long but side slit to her hip. Nothing could be more perfect for her entrance into the spotlight tonight.

As she walks toward me, I can tell she knows how desirable she looks, and the extra confidence makes her even more attractive. As my eyes travel her body, I notice the champagne stiletto heels and smile at the image of her wearing those later and nothing else. Although, it will be hard to ask her to remove this dress. I notice she is looking me up and down too and I raise an eyebrow. Most of the women I date don't bother. It's my money and power that draws them, not my looks. I have, of course, dressed for the occasion but nothing special. Just Armani. Still, as she reaches me, she smiles. "You look incredibly sexy tonight."

I chuckle. "No, you are the sexy one. Jesus. What a dress."

"I'm glad you approve," she says, a twinkle in her eyes. "You should see the back." Slowly, she turns, and I cannot help but growl in appreciation. The strapless plunging back is possibly the most tantalizing thing I have ever seen on her. My mouth longs to caress the bare skin. To kiss it. To nip it with my teeth. She looks at me over her shoulder. "Not too much?"

A throb between my legs is my first answer. It is indeed too much, but in the very best way, and under any other circumstance, I would push it up high enough to fuck her with my fingers while we stand by the pool. Unfortunately, I can't. Yet. "Definitely not too much," I finally answer her once I've caught my breath. "They will love it, and they will love you." Truly, I know this. I know what makes a star in this town. Her hair is down as a wavy cascade of gold. The makeup is subtle, except for the red lipstick. Just what she knows I want her to wear. I notice a glint and move closer. Modest dangling earrings. Midnight sapphires. I touch one. "I like these too."

She tilts her head. "I thought you might. You seem drawn to the color blue." A flash of last night and the ice-blue lingerie she wore while I took her comes immediately to mind, and I know that was her intention.

"I think you are right," I answer with a smile, moving in closer. "How perceptive of you." I put my hands on her hips to turn her back toward me, planning to kiss her, hard, but she puts her palms on my chest and stops me.

"Oh no you don't," she insists with a laugh. "You'll get lipstick everywhere." I am not sure what to say. No one refuses me, yet somehow, I like it. Claire is not afraid to say no to me. Still, she must notice I am unsure because she touches my bottom lip with the tip of her finger. It is sensual and does nothing to diffuse my wanting her. In another moment, I realize this is what she wants as she leans even closer to whisper in my ear. "But later, everywhere is where I want you. I promise."

---

27

*J*f Claire is nervous when she hits the red carpet outside of the Getty Museum, a person would never know it. Just as I predicted, the fans and reporters behind the velvet ropes lining the path are waiting for us. Questions pepper us, but as I suggested when we pulled up in the car, smiling and waving suffices for tonight. We can leak small tidbits in the weeks ahead, rather than a big splash interview, all as part of keeping a lower profile. Although there will be pictures of her on my arm everywhere. When Claire does smile at them, the paparazzi nearly swoon, and flashbulbs go off like fireworks. There is nothing quite as sought after as a fresh face in Hollywood.

"You are a natural," I whisper in her ear as we clear the gauntlet, and she laughs.

"I'm not so sure about that," she says holding tighter to my arm. "I was just focused on not tripping in these heels."

The thought of those gives me a tingle as I consider how they will come into play when we are back home later tonight, but before I can tell her, we are swept into the museum's grand foyer. People, industry-related mostly, are waiting for me. Some of them, I have not seen since this event last year, others even longer, and they suddenly want to catch up. I am not fooled. Everyone wants to get a closer look at my mystery woman. As I navigate the throngs of friends and foes alike, I introduce Claire again and again. She is gracious and lovely, and it makes me attracted to her all the more.

Finally, we find a quiet spot, and just when I think we are safely out of the limelight, someone catches my arm. When I look, it is Lila. "I didn't know you would be here," I say with raised eyebrows. Not that I am not pleased to see her. She makes me happy. "Why didn't you tell me?"

"A last-minute invitation," she replies with her always warm smile. "I offered to loan one of my Monet's to be in their next exhibit. Besides, I had to meet Claire." Of course, she wants to meet her. Lila is protective of me, has been since we became partners all those years ago. My friend, checking to ensure I'm not making a mistake, is exactly what I should have predicted.

"Claire, please meet Lila," I say. "One of my closest and dearest friends." Lila steps past me to close the distance between her and Claire, taking the woman by the hands, and kissing her on both cheeks.

"Such a pleasure," Lila says. "You are as lovely as I hoped. And your dress, my God, fantastic. I see why you are the talk of the evening." I watch Claire blush a little under the praise, but also give Lila a welcoming smile before she turns her eyes to me.

"Thank you. I picked it more for her than anyone."

Lila laughs, and I am relieved to hear it is sincere. A glance in my direction lets me know she is pleased with my choice, and I could not be happier. Although I would never admit it to anyone, the woman's approval means a great deal to me. "Then you are on the right track, my dear," Lila says with a wink showing her playful side which she disguises so well under her posh exterior. "Shall we find our spots for dinner? I see the wait staff making rounds asking people to be seated."

"Of course," I agree as Claire takes one of my arms. Lila takes the other, and I lead us to our seats. We are near the stage where there will be entertainment after we dine. I know the vocal artist well. She is one of my discoveries and turns me quite a profit with every new album. When the time comes for her to take the stage, after the dinner plates are whisked away, I am pleased to hear she is as good as the first day I saw her in a smoky bar in Indiana five years before. As I enjoy the start of her set, I feel a hand on my thigh, and a rush of heat blooms under the touch. If Claire wanted my attention away from the sexy entertainer gyrating on the stage, she has it. I lick my lips as her fingers travel higher. Sliding my hand under the table, I join Claire's only to have her take it and move the caress to her bare thigh. The slit in the dress is perfect for access to her leg, and I grit my teeth to keep from making a sound as she coaxes my hand between her legs. Nothing could turn me on more. I have touched women intimately on so many occasions, but I am usually the initiator. To have Claire lead me to where she wants me is a sensation I realize has been missing in my life. She is my sexual equal, and when I let my fingers graze the lace between her legs, it is her turn to squirm. Picking up her wine to take a sip to cover her arousal, I clear my throat as well but apply pressure where I know her hard clit nestles behind the fabric. Her wetness soaks through, and I want nothing than to have more access to what I know will be her swollen, slippery lips.

As she sets the wine glass down, her hand shakes a little,

and I force myself not to smile. "Good wine?" I ask at the same time I start to move my fingers in a small circle.

"Oh, yes," she gasps, and out of the corner of my eye, I notice Lila is watching us across the table. A knowing smile plays at the corners of her mouth, and I have no doubt she guesses at what we are doing under the table. I would also guess the idea of it turns her on as well. This only excites me more, and I slide the lace of Claire's panties to the side giving me access to Claire's center. The slightest moan of pleasure comes from her throat, covered by a high note from the singer on stage.

I lean in to whisper in her ear. "How quietly can you come?"

She turns to me, and I see the need for release in her eyes. "I think you know the answer to that," she murmurs in response. I chuckle moving my fingers lower until they slip inside her ever so slightly. I watch her face and see her bite her lip. The urge to kiss her mouth is strong, but I know not only Lila is watching. We are far too exciting a new couple not to attract some attention, even with a popstar belting out her latest number one hit on the stage.

"Do you want me to stop?" I tease, pulsing my hand back and forth, fucking her with two fingers just enough so I know I can make her come. All Claire can do is shake her head as her breathing turns heavy. Just then, the music dies down, and the singer stops to say a few words about how happy she is to have a chance to entertain for us. The timing for this lull could not be worse, and I watch as Claire closes her eyes to hold back. She lays her hands flat on the white linen tabletop to help steady herself. Stopping my thrusts, knowing even one more will do it, I have two choices. Keep going or remove my hand, leaving things unfinished. Unsure, I again see Lila who is smiling slyly and sipping her wine. Our eyes meet and hold. There is a twinkle of amusement in hers but a little touch of something else too. Regret, I think, but then it is gone.

"Wait for the applause, dear," she murmurs over the top of the glass, and I cannot help but give her a small smile in return for her excellent advice. As the entertainer finishes her speech with a sincere thank you people begin to clap. This is going to be most interesting indeed. As it grows louder, I start to move my hand again, and Claire sucks in a breath. Flexing my wrist, I plunge deeper, and it is precisely what she needs. Her mouth opens slightly in a small cry of release, and my body twitches with a hunger for her. We cannot get back to my estate soon enough, and I mentally curse the fact we have other business tonight. All I want to do right now is get on top of Claire and come as I thrust inside her.

As the music begins again, I move my hand back to the table and catch Lila looking at my fingers, her eyes half-lidded in what can only be described as lust. I know she is remembering times when I used them on her, and as much as that once pleased me, tonight makes me a touch sad for her. Those days we spent in bed together are gone even more permanently now. There is no one for me but the sexy, exciting Claire.

28

*I*rises. I gaze at the legendary painting by Van Gogh, while Claire stands beside me, her hand on my arm. Her confidence has yet to wane all night, whether faced with the paparazzi on the red carpet, to possibly deceiving a mastermind thief. There is more to her than meets the eye, and I look forward to exploring it all once this business is over. "Can I be honest?" she asks as she stares at the art.

I raise an eyebrow. "Always."

"It's kind of, well..." she turns to me. "Am I allowed to say I find it boring?"

I can't help but laugh. She's so refreshing, because I know there is probably no one else at this event who would say that out loud. I'm about to agree when I feel someone come up on the other side of me. Somehow, I know this is it and slowly turn, only to be wrong. "Lila," I say. "I thought you left." This could complicate matters a bit, and I quickly brainstorm different ways to send her away when she shakes her head.

"I'm sorry," she says, and I notice the same look of regret

in her eyes I saw before. It confuses me. She usually is so confident and in love with life. "My dear, please come with me. You need to talk to someone."

The reality of the situation hits me like a punch in the chest. Lila. Sweet, loving, considerate Lila. "No," I whisper. "Please say this isn't your doing."

"I don't understand," Claire says from beside me. "It's you?"

Not answering directly, Lila holds out her hand to me. "Please don't make this difficult. Just come with me."

I simply cannot believe it, but I take her hand to let her lead me away. Claire holds onto my arm. "Wait. Not without me."

"Claire—" I start, but she shakes her head. Determination is clear in her eyes.

"If you go, I go. We're a team."

I look to Lila. "I don't think it's a good idea," she says, but Claire will have none of it.

"Either I go with you right now, or I scream my head off and see what happens next."

Her threat is real, I know it. Lila sighs. "If you insist," she says. "But please hurry. We don't have much time."

We move as a group down a narrow, less conspicuous hallway with a few lesser-known paintings only to come to a door built into the wall. Unless a person is looking closely, it is undetectable in order to maintain the aesthetics of the gallery. Lila moves a small panel aside and keys in a code to unlock the door which opens inward. I pause, holding her hand so she must wait. "I can help you fix whatever it is making you do this," I tell her. My heart is breaking that she has anything to do with deceiving any of us.

"Actually, maybe you can do just that," a woman's voice calls from inside the private room. My curiosity piqued, I look over Lila's shoulder to see a small workroom. Boxes line one wall and a table with a stool sits at the center. A woman I've never met stands behind it although I do know her by reputation, and it is not a good one. She is taller than I realized, with dark hair to her shoulders, and a gorgeous face. She could easily have been a movie star or at least a model, but no, she is anything but that. Seeing my glare, she smiles broadly giving her face a sexy but sinister look. "Please, come in. No sense making a scene in the hallway."

I stride past Lila, leaving the other two women in my wake. Whatever bullshit is going on, I'm going to shut it down right now. "Georgia DeLane," I growl. "Why does this not surprise me? Or an even better question, how the hell did you get into this gala? No one in this town would lower themselves to inviting you."

Color rises to the woman's cheeks. My comments struck home, although there is nothing but truth behind it. Georgia is possibly as rich as I am, yet her money doesn't come from honest work, but rather from the blood and tears of people she crushed on her way to the top. Extortion, smuggling, even rumors of assassin for hire. Her involvement in the Dark Web underworld makes complete sense. It is exactly where someone like her belongs. The question is . . . how is Lila mixed up in it?

Claire and Lila come in behind me. "Close the door, Lila," Georgia growls, far less cordial. "Let's move this along."

"Yes, let's," I agree reaching into my jacket for the Bitcoin information. I see my adversary stiffen as if she thinks I am reaching for a weapon, and I laugh. "Relax. I'm not the criminal here. Where are the diamonds?" There is nothing visible on the table which would be big enough to hold as many gems as I've been advised to expect.

Georgia barks a laugh. "Oh, there are no diamonds. That is not what this is about. No, it was just to draw another of you out."

Furrowing my brow in confusion, I glance at Lila, but she won't meet my eye. Instead, Claire moves closer to me to lay a hand on my shoulder. "I think you should explain," she says, and I can tell from her tone she's not a fan of Georgia DeLane even though they just met. Her instinct is right not to trust the woman. She clearly has an agenda we are not privy to at the moment.

Georgia tilts her head regarding Claire, and the hungry look in her eyes makes the hair on the back of my neck rise in response. I clench and unclench my fists knowing she somehow trapped Lila and now has the audacity to eye my woman. Unfortunately, my response seems only to amuse Georgia and her smile widens. "Claire Hathaway," she coos. "A pleasure. Your dress is incredible, but the "come fuck me" stilettos really make it work."

"Shut your fucking mouth," I growl. "Just tell me why I'm here if it's not to buy diamonds."

"Fine," Georgia says with a wave of her hand. "There will be time for fun and games later." I don't care for the sound of that but keep quiet. I want things to move along. "I want in the club."

I glance at Lila. The club is a secret, and the fact Georgia DeLane knows about it at all is not good. "Oh, yes," Georgia says. "Your sweet friend let it slip one night after an especially good orgasm. Seems she thought she could trust me." My heart aches as I watch shame cross my friend's face. I believe Georgia though. It was under similar circumstances Lila recruited me for the club all those years before.

"Not on your life," I say without even bothering to look at the woman. The idea is so preposterous I would laugh under other circumstances. Our circle is based on trust and mutual admiration. We are each honest, respected business-women. The black-market world of Georgia DeLane is as far from our code as a person can get. "I'm shocked you'd even dare to ask."

A dark look crosses Georgia's face. "Why did you have to be the one to answer my offer? You're such an arrogant bitch." As she says it, I realize she doesn't know who else is in the club. She is using Lila as bait, and I look at my friend.

"You wouldn't tell her who we are," I murmur with renewed admiration. "So, she is using this desperate ploy to lure us out." I have to laugh. Zena, Kris, Chloe, and the others were extra careful in making their inquiries on the Dark Web just in case this was a trap. They were so right.

Lila finally looks up. "I'm so sorry. I was a fool." My heart goes out to her, and clearly, Claire feels it too as she crosses to her and puts an arm around her shoulders.

"You are a victim, nothing else," she says shooting daggers at Georgia. The woman chuckles, and I hate the sound of it.

She looks at me. "Wherever did you find her?" she asks. "Absolutely exquisite. And I saw you at the table. During the performance, you fucked her, didn't you?"

I don't think but instead, react and dive across the table to choke the evil woman standing there. She blocks me easily. A lifetime of crime has taught her well. Even enraged, I am a poor challenge. As she wraps a hand around my throat and forces me against the wall, I see more than anger in her eyes. There is jealousy. She wants what I have—respect, friends, allies, love. This is what she thinks the club will bring her. Things she will never have on her own and clearly hopes to take by force.

"Last chance," she hisses in my face. "Extend an invitation and sponsor me, or else."

For a fleeting moment, I think she is threatening to kill me, but then the reality of the situation hits me. She doesn't want me dead. I am her possible in, and there are things she can do that will hurt me more. Letting me go, I choke for air but reach for her to stop what I know is about to happen. Georgia brushes me aside and knocks on a different door, which no doubt leads to the greater warehouse supporting the museum. A man dressed as a security officer opens it. "Yes, ma'am?" he asks, and I know he has been bought off if he is not an imposter all together.

Georgia waves in my direction. "Escort her out to the main group. She is ready to leave for the night."

The man nods and glances at where Claire and Lila stand together. "And these two?"

I watch with my heart in my throat as Georgia takes a silenced handgun from inside her jacket. "They are coming with me." She throws me a wink. "I'm in the mood for a threesome."

29

"*T*his is not over," I growl as the security guard puts a hand on my shoulder and starts to push me toward the exit. "If you take them, I will use every resource I have to find you and destroy you."

Georgia rolls her eyes at my threat. "Have fun with that," she says. "But all you have to do is tell me who the other members of your group are, and we can all go home happy. Just let me in your little club."

I am full of indecision. The idea of letting Claire, as well as Lila, go with her is killing me, but there is no telling what Georgia will do with the information she wants. This could be about more than being a part of the club. Blackmail of any of the closeted lesbians among us is no doubt on her agenda. Some of them could lose everything if the truth comes out. Some could even die. I know I cannot trust her, but I also cannot walk away from Claire either.

Before I decide, Claire leaves Lila's side and comes around the table to me. I have no idea what she is thinking. It's a bold and crazy move and my heart pounds at the risk she is taking. "What the fuck are you doing?" Georgia asks with a frown, but Claire ignores her and when she reaches me, takes my face in her hands. Still confused, I start to ask her a question, but then she kisses me. There is more than tenderness there. Her mouth is hungry for me, and I respond without thinking of anything but her. The unbridled passion runs between us, and I only feel her mouth on mine. Then, as suddenly as she started, she pulls back and looks hard into my eyes.

"Don't tell this bitch anything," she says. "We will be okay until you find us. And I know you will." She turns away from me and returns to Lila's side again, not even bothering to look in Georgia's direction. Jesus, this woman is brave and strong and everything I could ever hope to find in one person, all the more reason I must do something.

Georgia narrows her eyes. "Cute," she says, then she waves her handgun toward the door leading to the gallery hallway. "Okay, no more, off you go. Before anyone wonders where you went." Again, the guard pushes me, and I shrug him off.

"I can walk." We go together out the exit, and as the door closes behind me, I struggle to keep calm. Claire and Lila are in great danger, and I'm walking away. Anything could happen to them. I need to do something. The security guard is not armed, and I wonder if I could subdue him when I notice a painting across from us. I don't know the name of the more obscure artist, but if the thing is here, it is valuable. In two strides, I reach it and yank the frame to tear the painting from the wall. The minute I start to pull, alarms scream.

"What are you doing?" the guard asks yelling over the sirens. "Are you nuts?" He starts to look around, no doubt realizing he is about to be caught. Even if he really is a guard, I'll be sure to explain why he is with me. I'm respected enough to be believed, and he clearly knows it. "Fuck." The man runs leaving me alone to rush back to the locked door in the wall. There is no time to screw around with trying to figure out the code, and I slam my shoulder into it. There is a creak, and I am grateful the door opens inward an inch giving me a chance. Stepping back, I kick at the lock. Once, twice, and on the third time, it crashes open. Shouts to stop sound from behind me, but I do not hesitate to plunge inside. Claire and the others are gone, but the second door out to the warehouse is open.

Pushing past the table, I race into the space beyond the door and see a wooden staircase leading down to a broad concrete pad with wooden boxes and palettes everywhere. At the bottom, about to turn a corner, I see Georgia DeLane forcing the other two women forward by gunpoint. "Hey," I yell, taking the steps two at a time. "Stop!" Georgia turns on her heel and without a word, raises her weapon. I duck just as a bullet whizzes over my head to send splinters from the steps above me spinning away.

"That was a warning shot," she hisses. "Now fuck off." I don't. She can shoot me, even kill me, but I won't let her take Claire and Lila. I wait for another shot, but instead, Georgia pushes the women forward. "Hurry up. We have a ride to catch." They disappear around the corner as I leap the last few steps to land hard on the concrete floor. I stumble to the wall at the edge of the corner and lean on it to breathe for a second. My heart is racing, and I know going blind around the corner is probably a death sentence. She could be right there, ready to blow my head off.

"Shit," I whisper. This could be it, the end of my life and for a fleeting moment, I think how much that sucks, because I only just found Claire. We are so good together, and our future looks magical. That thought is enough to make me brave, because I won't let her go without a fight. I mentally count to three and then dash around the corner only to find a wide hallway, big enough to allow for a panel truck to back in to deliver supplies. At the end of the corridor, there is a rolling garage door, and as I watch, the three women walk out the exit into the night. Even though I hear the sound of sirens approaching, if Georgia has a car waiting, I will be too late.

Breaking out into a run, I close the distance only to see my fears confirmed. A black van waits at the loading dock, and someone inside is sliding the side door open. In a moment, Georgia will have them inside and be gone. "Claire!" I yell needing her to know I will come for her and when she turns to look, I am horrified to watch her stumble. The stiletto heels fail her, and she drops to her hands and knees. This is the delay I need, and I race toward them, not caring what happens to me.

Georgia sees me coming and raises her gun. "That's it," she snarls. "You're too much a pain in the ass to work with." I'm about to die. I'm an easy target as I charge her, but I don't care if it will save the others. Help is coming. All I need to do is delay her.

"No," Lila cries from beside Georgia suddenly grabbing the woman's arm and wrestling for the gun.

"Lila, don't," I yell, but the weapon fires, and Lila stumbles away. I have no idea if the bullet hit her, but the handgun falls and skitters across the concrete driveway. My instinct is to catch Lila before she collapses, which is all Georgia needs to step into the van. The sirens are close, and she will be lucky to escape even if she leaves now.

With her hand on the sliding door, she stares at me where I stand with Lila in my arms. "You're right," she says. "This is definitely not over. Watch yourself. I'll be back." She punctuates her words by slamming closed the van door as the vehicle squeals its tires to race away to escape. A police squad car is coming toward them, and I am happy to know it's over. She waited too long to go. Georgia will be arrested, and I will ensure she pays for her crimes. Only the van doesn't slow, and even when the police veer into her path, Georgia's driver broadsides the front of the car, plowing past it to keep going. Watching in disbelief, the black van races off into the night and disappears. Georgia is gone.

Suddenly, Claire is beside me. "Are you hurt?" she asks, and I notice tears in her eyes. I want to pull her in close, but I am still holding a trembling Lila.

"I'm okay. She missed me," I answer lowering Lila to sit on the curb. "Lila, are you okay?"

The older woman nods. "I think so. Might be having a heart attack though," she says with a shaky laugh, but then puts her face in her hands. "I am so sorry about this. You and Claire could have died."

I sink down beside her. "The woman used you. When you figured that out, she left you with no choice. But it's over. We know what she is up to and can stop her."

Lila looks at me, and I can tell from her eyes she doesn't believe me. To be honest, I don't believe it either. We have not seen the last of Georgia DeLane.

30

$\mathcal{W}$hen my car finally drops us back at my home in the hills above the ocean, it is well past midnight. The police detectives wanted to know every detail of our interaction with Georgia DeLane. She apparently is a challenging person to get a bead on, and the fact she was at the Getty Museum for the gala made all the law enforcement on the premises excited. To them, it confirmed she is in Los Angeles, although I don't believe it for a second. The woman is far too smart to be trapped anywhere. No doubt she is well on her way to the other side of the globe to some hideaway in Thailand or someplace welcoming to criminals. At least, that is what I would be doing if I were in her shoes.

Of course, it didn't help matters that the three of us can't really explain why Georgia was interested in our being there. Bringing up anything to do with the club during the interviews was out of the question. Although there was no time to warn Claire, it wasn't necessary. It turns out she was as evasive as Lila or me. In the end, the detectives were frustrated, and if we were anyone else, we might have been taken downtown for more questioning. Eventually, they had enough and sent us home. I offered to let Lila stay at the estate, but she declined.

"I'm so embarrassed," she admitted. "All I want to do is have a bottle of wine and a hot bath to wash all this off." After kisses all around, we watched her whisk away in a taxi.

Claire leaned on my arm with her head on my shoulder. "I am so thankful you are safe," she whispered, and I kissed her forehead.

"Same," I said and called for my car to come to get us.

Now, as we walk through the foyer of the mansion, all I want to do is take Claire in my arms and hold her close—to convince myself she is safe. As if knowing my thoughts, she drops the heels she carried all night and falls into me. I wrap her up, and we stand in silence for a moment as we process the fact everything is all right, and we are here, safe together. The realization makes me thankful to be alive. I could have lost my life tonight, although it makes my stomach hurt more to think I might have lost Claire. My brave, beautiful, sexy Claire.

As I hold her, the familiar stirring of excitement starts inside me. Her body feels so good against mine and the thrill of surviving tonight lingers. Running my hands up her back, I feel the warmth and softness of her naked skin. The backless dress. So incredibly sexy all night and she made it clear it was all for me. The memory of touching her under the table makes me catch my breath, and I know Claire feels my body posture changing as she turns her head to let me kiss her. I touch her lips gently with mine. There is a tenderness between us for a moment as we nuzzle each other's faces, sharing soft kisses. My heart is full, and my emotions for her are strong, almost to the point of scaring me a little. If anything had happened to her...

Realizing how close things came to ending horribly, my

next kiss is deeper. I need to feel her passion, if only for a moment before I take her upstairs to sleep. We are both tired, although I know the leftover adrenaline will keep me awake for hours still. Something about being shot at while trying to rescue my lover is a bit much to compartmentalize. Later I will process all of it, but for now, the thrill lingers, and my kiss contains some of that.

As if feeling the same, Claire kisses me back with equal passion and our kiss deepens. Suddenly, the heat replaces the tenderness, and she runs her hands into my hair to pull me in closer. The sensation of her hunger for me sends a charge of desire through my body, and I wrap my arms around her waist to hold her tight against me feeling every curve of her through the thin material of the black dress. As her lips part, inviting me in, I use my tongue to conquer her mouth, and she moans a little cry of pleasure. No one can possibly kiss like we do, so perfect for each other, fitting so seamlessly. Breaking the kiss, we rest our foreheads together, each breathing heavy. "I want you," I tell her, and she nods.

"I want you too." She pauses, as if hesitant to say what she is thinking before telling me her desires in a whisper. "And I want you to take me like you did on the ship." I grit my teeth to contain the rush of desire that threatens to over-whelm me at her words. Fucking her tonight, when I am still charged from all that happened and almost happened, is exactly what I want to do. It's as if she can read me, and I intend to reward her for it.

"Keep your dress on," I say taking her hand and leading her outside to the pool. The sky is filled with the last hints of moonlight before it dips below the horizon and brings on the dawn. "One minute."

She nods, a gleam of anticipation in her eyes. With a last

kiss, deep and hungry, I leave her for a moment only to return with what she wants under my slacks. She is perched on the end of an oversized cushioned lounger and watches me as I walk across the patio to her. There is desire in her eyes, but something else too. It's as if while I was gone, she missed me and not because I have money and power, but because I'm me.

Catching my breath at the idea, I suddenly want to do more than take her on the cushions, but to make love to her. To make her feel so entirely consumed she will never think of anyone else. "Come here," I tell her as I undo my belt and pull down my zipper.

I watch as she licks her lips at my actions. "God, you are so sexy," she says as she walks to me. Her body in the incredible dress is what is sexy. I suck in a deep breath and when she is close, take her by the hips to pull her against me. When she brushes my strap-on, I watch her face. Her eyes half close as she presses harder into me, and I know she wants to feel me as much as I want to be inside her.

Taking her face in my hands, I kiss her, slow but deep and passionate. She shivers and then gasps when I break away. I can tell she is as caught up in the moment as I am, feeling everything with so much more intensity because of tonight's danger. Wanting more, I slide my hand up the bare thigh inside the slit of her dress. The skin is hot and smooth making me hungry for her. I slowly pull up the black fabric to reach under it with my other hand until it is at her hips, and I cup her backside to grind her against me again. Feeling what I have waiting for her, she grabs my shirt in her fists and lets out a small cry of excitement. The sound drives me crazy, and I lower us to the edge of a lounger until I sit on the cushions while pulling her to straddle me. With a thigh on each side of my hips, she grinds against me again and the pressure of what

I am wearing rubs my clit. I can't suppress a moan. "Jesus, you feel good on top of me," I growl starting to lose my restraint.

Looping my thumbs through the back of her lace panties, I rip and tear them into pieces watching her eyes widen with surprise as I pull the fabric free, leaving her exposed. "How do you always know what will drive me crazy?" she breathes. I smile and lay back until I can look up at her. Nothing restricts her movement now, and she immediately starts to rock her hips back and forth running her swollen lips over the bulge of what I am wearing.

"Touch me," I demand and with a moan, she does what I ask, reaching and freeing the shaft from my pants. She grips it at the base, and I grit my teeth, knowing she understands what I want next. "Put me inside you."

"Oh God," she says tilting her head back as she rises up just enough to slide me in.

Using every ounce of my control, I hold perfectly still. "Slowly," I instruct her.

She nods, lowering herself all the way down until she is against my hips again, and I know I have filled her completely. "You are so deep," she moans. "No one's ever made me feel like this." Knowing it's true, I can't keep from lifting my hips to drive even deeper. "Oh my God. You're incredible." She starts to rock back and forth, in control of how hard or fast she wants to be fucked. I take her by the hips, holding her tight against me, but letting her dictate the pace.

"This is all you," I tell her, and her answer is to grind down harder and rock back and forth faster. Her blonde hair hangs down her back, and her chest heaves with an uncontrollable need. Knowing she is close to tipping, I slide my hands up her body to push aside the narrow strip of fabric covering her breasts and find her hard nipples with my fingers. Pulling and teasing, she arches her back and begins to shake.

"Can I come?" she begs, and as my own pleasure mounts, I love knowing she wants me to give her permission.

"Wait for me."

"I want to come with you," she whimpers.

The sound of her begging is all I need to climax, and as the first roll of my orgasm starts, I lift my hips again to go deeper. "Come with me."

With a scream of release that I know comes from her core, she rocks even faster, driving down on me to take every last bit. "Yes," she screams. "Yes, oh God, yes."

As the waves roll over us, and I hang on to her, she suddenly covers her face with her hands and starts to shake. It takes a moment to register she is sobbing. "Claire," I say sitting up onto my elbows, worried I hurt her with our love-making. "What's wrong?" Shifting my hips, I leave her body while I pull her down on top of me. Wrapping my arms tight around her, she snuggles her face into my neck, and I feel the wet of tears on her face. I hate this. I don't understand. "Please, talk to me." After another minute, her crying slows, and she wipes at her face.

"I'm sorry," she says with a sob still in her voice. "I didn't expect that."

I smooth a lingering tear away with my thumb. "What happened?"

She takes in a ragged breath. "I thought I was going to lose you tonight. And I couldn't stand it." I feel tears burn my own eyes at her confession. I felt the same yet am not sure what to do with the feelings. Then I hear her say words

I have never really registered before. Not with anyone. "I think I've fallen in love with you."

My chest tightens at the confession. Anxiety, but also happiness, makes my heart beat faster. As I think of all that has happened between us, I realize one thing is real through it all. My feelings for Claire. "I feel the same," I whisper. "I love you."

31

Kissing Claire on the lips, I shrug on my leather jacket and prepare to leave the hotel room. "I have to go," I say. "I'm sorry I can't take you with me, but—"

She cuts me off with another kiss. "Don't. I understand. Go." I smile and hurry out. My helicopter waits on the roof to take me to a destination I can't disclose to her. The club is meeting to discuss all that happened over the last month, including what to do with Lila. It is not a meeting I dare miss. In the two weeks since the night where Claire and Lila were nearly abducted, and I was almost shot, things have been a whirlwind. Not only must I catch up on business dealings, which I have been too distracted to handle personally, but there is Claire. After processing my love for her the night by the pool, I will not let her out of my sight for long. This means shuttling back and forth between Chicago and Los Angeles. I've even met her brother and mom. Meeting a woman's family was a first for me. I think they are still leery of my intentions, which is fair considering my reputation. Time will show them my love for Claire is quite real.

Long talks and nights wrapped in each other's arms beside my pool, watching the sunset, have led us to come to some conclusions. For one, we love each other, but also barely know each other. Even though it has been hard, very hard, we slowed things down, and I am romancing her as I should have from the beginning. I am already hoping for more, even marriage, but Claire can take all the time she needs.

For another, Claire agreed to move to Los Angeles and stay with me, in her own suite of rooms for now. No strings attached. We visit each other's beds often, but again, I am patient. She is worth it. I am convinced there is no one else for me and when I see the members of the club later, especially Zena, I look forward to telling them so. Their demand that I settle down and keep out of the spotlight is easy to meet. As my helicopter whisks me away, I wonder if it was not all somehow destined.

As I arrive at the old mining town miles outside of the city, I consider this one of the best hiding places we have at our disposal. Inside the retired mine itself is an elaborate bunker Chloe constructed at the recent turn in world political events. "Just in case," she told us, and none of us could blame her. The place is more like a retreat, and the day would be a good one if not for such dire topics to discuss. Georgia DeLane has not been apprehended. In fact, there have been no sightings or word of her location, even though we are all using our resources to find the woman. Her layers of protection thanks to the underworld where she resides are formidable, and frankly, scary knowing we are all prone to be a target especially.

Going through three rounds of security, which I worry at some point is going to be a body cavity search Chloe is being so thorough, I finally get to the meeting to find the entire group is in attendance. All twelve members. My eyes find Lila, and she is pale, no doubt afraid she is about to be expelled from a group she helped found and loves with all her heart. Going to sit beside her, I take her hand and give it a squeeze of support. I am on her side, and she smiles at me gratefully.

"Glad you could make it," Chloe starts, a touch of sarcasm in her voice. It's typical, so all I do is smile.

"I've been distracted lately. Lots of business to catch up on." A few in the group chuckle. My love life is no secret among the members.

Zena clears her throat. "Let's start with that order of business then," she says. "Seems you lived up to your debt. From all reports, Claire is quite charming. Well done."

I try not to be insulted. For Zena, there is no such thing as love, only arrangements. "She's amazing," I answer. "And I love her." More smiles around the table, including a wry one from Chloe. She's another who doesn't believe in love, but for different reasons. Her past haunts her, and only I know the whole truth about the girl who got away.

"More difficult to discuss though," Zena continues, drawing my attention back to the meeting, "is Lila." She turns to the woman, and I feel her grip my hand tighter. "You've put everyone at great risk."

Lila nods, and I see a touch of shine to her eyes. Tears, but I know she will never let them fall. She may be heart broken over what is happening, but she is still the classiest most put-together woman I have ever known. "I know," she answers. "And I am willing to accept whatever the group decides."

"Then, we will vote. Everyone has been briefed. Your affair with Georgia DeLane and disclosing information about the existence of our club."

"But not who is in it," I jump in. "Even at the end, with a gun in her face, she would not betray any of us." There is a hush in the room as everyone digests this information.

Finally, Zena nods. "We will vote," she says. "Right now and be done with this business, so we can focus on what to do with our new problem." I take a breath and hold it. This is it, and I will be as heartsick as Lila if she is asked to leave us. "A show of hands. Who feels Lila should be expelled from the group for her indiscretions?"

Four people raise their hands, including Zena and Val. I make eye contact with Chloe, who shrugs and keeps her hand down. Exhaling with relief, I put an arm around Lila to give her a hug. She can stay. "But may I suggest probation of some sort?" Yuki suggests, even though she did not vote against her. "Perhaps no lovers for a year? To be safe?"

Lila blushes at the comment but also nods. "I will agree to it."

"Then it is settled," Zena says with a small sigh that I recognize is relief. Even voting against Lila, they are friends, and Zena would be sad to see her go. Only Val looks genuinely irritated by the outcome, and I make a mental note to keep it in mind while Zena continues. "Now, let's move on to our last topic. This one will take longer to fix, I'm afraid."

A murmur goes around the room. "If at all," Kris adds under her breath and this scares me. If the technical genius in the group is unsure, we are all probably screwed.

Zena nods at Kris' statement. "Indeed, we have a dangerous adversary," she says. "Georgia DeLane."

THE END

ABOUT THE AUTHOR

KC Luck is a bestselling indie author of multiple lesbian fiction novels to include *The Darkness Trilogy* and many short stories. Her books cross multiple genres and she is an Amazon bestseller in lesbian romance, lesbian erotica, LGBT horror, LGBT science fiction, and LGBT action & adventure. She is currently working on the sequel to TLBC.

Regardless of plot, all of KC Luck's novels focus on strong female leads in loving lesbian relationships.

To receive updates on KC Luck's books, please consider subscribing to her mailing list (http://eepurl.com/dx_iEf). Also, KC Luck is always thrilled to hear from readers (kc.luck.author@gmail.com) . Website – www.kc-luck.com

ALSO BY KC LUCK

Rescue Her Heart

Rescue Her Heart Audiobook

Save Her Heart

Welcome to Ruby's

Darkness Falls

Darkness Falls Audiobook

Darkness Remains

Darkness Remains Audiobook

Darkness United

Darkness United Audiobook

The One

Naughty List

Printed in Great Britain
by Amazon

79248375R00103